I0612103

The Feeder

Gayle Siebert

Published by Idyllbeck Opportunities, 2023.

Also by Gayle Siebert

Lindy Larsen
After The Dance
Katawasis Girls
The Bones Below

Lisa Rogney
Call Me Lisa
Wembly

Secrets
The Bear Mountain Secret
The Spirit Bear Secret
The Dark River Secret

Standalone
Where The Mule Grazed
The Feeder

Watch for more at https://www.gaylesiebert.com.

Table of Contents

One

Carly

Morning breath bothers Derek, so when I finally hear him stirring in the bedroom overhead, I go into the powder room and scrub my teeth for the second time. I use enough toothpaste to foam up and nearly gag myself to ensure my breath is minty fresh.

When I come back into the kitchen he's there, back to me, pouring a cup of coffee. "Good morning," I say, and come to stand beside him. "You're late getting up."

He gives me a sideways glance and mumbles something that's probably "good morning." Shirtless and barefoot, sweatpants hanging low on his hips, he doesn't turn to face me or put his arm around me, but stands at the sink gazing out the window, surveying the backyard.

It's really all I expect. He's not a morning person. Early in our relationship he explained he needs at least one cup of coffee and a little quiet time before he feels human. For me, it's the best time of the day. For one thing, this is when we sometimes have a good morning I-love-you kiss. Saturdays and Sundays are the most special. I'm hoping this morning he'll suggest we take our coffee upstairs and lock the bedroom door. Jennifer is old enough to let her parents "sleep in" on weekends. I stroke his shoulder and murmur, "We could take our coffee and go back to bed..."

"What the..." Derek has spotted something out the window. He shrugs me off, puts his cup down, and races through the family room and out the patio door, swearing loudly. I grit my teeth. I wish he would keep his voice down, especially this early. The neighbors might hear. Language like that, and on a Sunday to boot!

I go to the door and watch as he bends over the bird feeder, now a mess of scattered wood pieces and seeds on the patio. It must have come down during the windstorm that swept through overnight. It looks ruined. Could this be the end of the darn thing at last?

No hug or kiss, but I still feel a rush of joy.

Two

Lita

I'm slowly coming awake. I don't want to open my eyes, not yet, because opening them would mean waking up too fast. I crack open one eye just so I can check the clock radio on the table beside me. 7:30. It's Sunday morning. I don't have to get out of bed this early. What woke me? Then I smell coffee and realize the other side of the bed is messed up. Oh yeah. Nullah. Last night. I hear him humming now.

In moments, Nullah appears in the doorway. The sight of the man, solid muscle and buck naked and with a steaming mug in each hand, is what I can only describe as astonishing. He's athletic, a bodybuilder for no reason other than he likes to keep fit and admires the bodybuilder physique. Makes sense. The guy is the Canadian distributor for a couple of workout equipment manufacturers and owns half a dozen fitness clubs and gyms.

Besides being wide at the shoulder and narrow at the hip, he's well-endowed in another important area and jaw-droppingly handsome besides, largish nose notwithstanding. Much as I've never liked tattoos, I'm even getting used to the intricate and quite beautiful Māori one that covers his left shoulder and part of his chest. At the moment, it's the mugs I'm interested in, though.

"Good morning, beautiful," he says as he comes up to me and sets a mug on the bedside table.

"Good morning," I mutter. It's difficult to match his enthusiasm. I'm a little annoyed that he's waking me up this early on a Sunday, but bringing me coffee in bed mostly makes up for it. I sit up, tuck the sheet around me, lift the mug and take a few sips. I start to mellow out as the warmth floods through me.

"Your neighbor was out walking that little dog of hers," he says. "She saw me in the window and waved."

"She saw you?"

"In the kitchen window. Not the big window."

"Well maybe next time, go to the big window and give the old girl a thrill," I suggest, knowing Irene might have a coronary if he actually did it.

Nullah laughs, goes around to the other side of the bed and climbs up to sit next to me. After a few more sips, I ask, "Why are you up so early? More to the point, why did you wake me up?"

"The bite at Sisters Island is at nine, so we need to get moving. By the time we're out on the water—"

"Fishing?"

"We talked about this last night."

It's coming back to me. "I don't think I agreed, though, did I?"

"You didn't say no."

"Implied consent because I didn't say anything when everyone was talking? You know I don't like fishing."

"Well, it's a beautiful day. Don't worry, it'll be dead calm on the water. No chance of getting seasick on such a calm morning."

"That's what you think."

"I thought we'd fish, just for a couple of hours, before we go to meet the others at the Dinghy Dock for lunch."

"Hmmm." Oh yeah, now I remember someone talking about the Dinghy Dock. That's probably what I agreed to, because I love that place. A ten-minute boat ride across the channel to tie up at the floating pub. Drinks and pub grub with the waves lapping the deck is one of the best things about living here. We could spend the whole afternoon there, and when we come back, get a waffle cone and stroll along the seawall before going home. It sounds light years better than going to Carly's.

I wish I hadn't accepted Carly's invitation to dinner, but I had run out of excuses, especially when she changed the invitation from Saturday to Sunday because I said I had a conflict. No doubt it'll be some over-the-top display of her cooking chops, fancy china, and crystal glasses. It's what she loves to do. I get that, and I guess I should be supportive, but is it too late to cancel? I mull it over and realize I would feel guilty if I jammed out now.

"I have to be at Carly's at four."

"Yeah. Carly. I've been wondering. She's married, right? So it's not just the two of you. Why didn't she suggest you bring me? Er, a date? Or why didn't you suggest it?"

"Nullah, don't feel bad about it. I quit taking a boyfriend with me to dinners with them years ago."

"Oh, yeah? Why?"

"It's just, um, hard to explain. It's awkward. They'd make you feel uncomfortable. Her husband, Derek. Derek would make you feel uncomfortable."

"I can take it."

"I can't."

"Then why don't you invite them to go with us to the Dinghy Dock? That way, if he does something that makes you uncomfortable I can toss the fucker overboard. Her too, so there wouldn't be any witnesses."

There's a twinkle in his eye. We share a grin. I tell him, "They'd likely bring their kid."

"Hmmm. That would be a problem."

"Not really. If you think you wouldn't want to toss her overboard along with the other two, that's only because you haven't met her. Anyway, if I know Carly, she's already started on dinner, and believe me, she would not welcome a change of plans."

"You haven't told them about me, have you." It's not a question.

"Well, umm, actually, no." At his frown, I continue, "But don't take it personally." I put my mug down and get out of bed, heading for the bathroom. In the doorway, I turn back to face him and say, "I haven't seen them since you and I got together, you know."

"You're Facebook friends, aren't you?"

"Sure, but I'm more of a lurker on other people's posts. I don't post any personal stuff. You know that." I wonder why he's pursuing this. Does he really think I'd Facebook-announce to the world that we're dating? It's only been a couple of months. I need to wait and see if it goes anywhere before I change my relationship status.

"I've told all my friends. Hell, you've met all my friends. You could've at least mentioned me in one of your texts," he says.

"We don't text all that often. And they're short. Just *hi, how r u doing* and I reply, *good. You?*" He doesn't look mollified, so I continue, "I'll tell them about you tonight. I'll suggest meeting them for drinks sometime so they can get to know you. Somewhere that we can make a quick getaway so we don't have to drown anyone."

Maybe I should tell him that every time I've taken a boyfriend to Carly's, Derek acts like a cornered rat, or more accurately, an alpha male dog. Another alpha male like Nullah showing up would really start him snarling. He'd feel so intimidated and threatened he'd probably tell one of his racist jokes. There would be no good guy act like he puts on for the ladies. Or at least used to. I don't remember the last time I saw them in a group setting.

Once I'm finished in the bathroom and get back in bed, I study Nullah's face. He's appeased by my suggestion we double date with the Wiltons, but judging by the set of his jaw, only slightly.

"Okay, then," he agrees. After a moment, he puts his hand on my arm and gently strokes it. "So about today. How about we forget fishing and just tour around the islands a little bit, have a couple of Bailey's coffees, then hit the Dinghy Dock early enough to get you back here in time."

"Perfect! And while we're doing that, I really wouldn't mind watching you fish. For a little while."

"That's my girl," he murmurs, and slips an arm around my shoulders.

I snuggle up closer to him, careful not to spill my coffee. He squeezes me and kisses my temple. I wonder if I'm in love.

Three

Carly

I'm chopping onions, preparing to cook lunch. This must be a particularly strong onion because it's really burning my eyes and my nose is running like a tap. I pull another Kleenex out of the dispenser on the window ledge over the sink, dab my eyes, then blow loudly.

My gaze drifts out the window. There's Derek, fussing over that bird feeder. I hear myself sigh. He's been to RONA to get what he needed, and now he'll spend the rest of the day fixing the darn thing. Before long it'll be dangling from the walnut tree again.

Years ago, on the day he hung that first feeder, I asked, can't you put it at the back of the yard? Why put it on that tree? Aren't we going to replace it with a magnolia or something more attractive? That darn thing's messy: half dead, always dropping branches, and when it drops the nuts, it attracts those noisy, squawking blue jays.

His response? They're not blue jays, they're Stellar's Jays.

The walnut tree not only stayed, but kept growing. Each fall the walnuts drop, the noisy jays show up at the crack of dawn, pry the nuts out, and leave a mess of shells and pods that stain the cement if they're not cleaned up right away. And the bird feeder adds to the mess with all the seeds scattered around.

The whole yard would go to wrack and ruin if it was left to Derek. He wants everything to look ship-shape, but I'm the one who pulls weeds and cleans up under the trees, and scrubs the stains off the patio.

Now he's out there on a ladder putting up the new, more secure system for hanging the feeder, making sure it can't fall again. Finished, he gets down off the ladder, folds it up, and takes it into the garage.

Watching him, shirtless and in shorts, I still can't believe that beautiful man is my husband. He's tanned and toned and still has that six-pack. When I met him, it was just his natural physique. Now he has to spend several nights a week at the gym to keep it.

He hasn't changed. Not at all, in ten years. Well, not physically anyway. Between the bird houses and his recent interest in boating, we hardly talk to each other anymore. Now when he's not on his phone or iPad searching out ideas for bird houses, he's finding out everything he can about boats.

The bird feeder was only the beginning. He spent weeks—months even—building detailed replicas of famous houses, for birds to live in. Several have cupolas and working weathervanes. They became so fancy that they're too nice to go out in the yard. Small ones, big ones, modern, colonial style, they clutter up the mantel, every vacant spot on the bookshelves, every window ledge. Dust collectors!

When he quit spending so much time on bird houses, I took it as a good sign. Maybe we could do something as a couple. Or as a family. Travel maybe. Then he got interested in boats. Now I wish he'd go back to building bird houses.

Until his boat craze when he decided to restore the wharf in front of our house and the steps on the steep trail leading down to it, he built little things, not big things. He didn't get around to fencing the yard until last year, too late to keep little Jennifer from wandering off, so I had to watch her constantly to prevent her toppling down the bank. He might never have built the fence if he hadn't hoped it would keep Jeff and Linda's cats out of our yard and away from the birds. Didn't work, of course.

I was friendly with next-door neighbors when they first moved in, though from day one Derek thought Jeff was an asshole and pronounced them low class. When they refused to keep their cats out of our yard, the arguments started. The cats are still a bone of contention, so we're not friendly with them despite living next to them all this time.

The neighbors on our other side moved in last year. They don't have cats but they go back and forth to Jeff and Linda's and sit out on their patio visiting and laughing, probably at us. They are not people we need to know.

At first I thought building bird houses was interesting and something I might try my hand at. Something we could do together. But women, in general, don't have the spatial recognition ability for it and it's obvious from how I would arrange furniture if left to my own devices that I certainly don't. As for boating, something else we might do together as a family, he prefers to go for an hour or so just when I'm getting dinner ready or clearing up after. Jennifer goes with him more often than I do.

I have mentioned to him that his daughter is growing up, and he knows more about boats, bird feeders and bird houses, than what's going on in her life. He said he knows very well what's going on in Jennifer's life and points out they have quality one-on-one time on the boat, and also that he's the one that goes to her soccer games and music lessons and teacher interviews. What do I do? Drop her off at the pool or at her friend's house, that's it. End of discussion.

I don't begrudge him his hobbies. His job is stressful, and he works long hours. He needs quiet time to unwind, so he either takes the boat out, goes to the gym, or works in the garage. Only a useless wife would expect her husband to come home after a hard day at the office and take on the job of running a household, and I am not a useless wife.

I wipe my eyes with a cool, wet paper towel, then scrape the diced onions into the frying pan along with chopped celery and bacon. I adjust the temperature and stir as the mixture sautés. Next, I add a can of drained and rinsed kidney beans and a dollop of sour cream.

Derek doesn't have a name for this dish, other than "those beans". It's more than just beans; it's a complete lunch, to be served with cottage cheese and French fries. Early in our marriage he told me he wanted it once a week. His first wife didn't like to cook and refused to touch an onion. She told him if he wanted those beans so badly, he could make them himself. Of course, cutting up onions is a stinky, eye-stinging job, but I like doing things that please Derek, and besides, I'm way more compliant than his first wife. The fact I'm easygoing is what first attracted him to me, he said. I know I'm not perfect, but I try, and we're still together, ten years on.

Derek looks the same as he did when we married, but I've put on a few pounds over the years. He says his first wife was slim. I tell him I, too, was slim when I was nineteen. Also his first wife never had a baby. He speaks of her so seldom you'd think she never existed, but when he does, it's as if she was perfect in every way despite never making him his beans. It's tragic she died so young, so I suppose it's no wonder. Still, sometimes I feel like I don't measure up. I started packing on the pounds in college and I never lost the baby weight, but I do make him his beans. Besides that, no one can be a gourmet cook and skinny, too. Mom always told me: cook your man happy.

My best friend, Lita, is skinny. Lita and I were roommates back in the day. She married before Derek and I did, but never really settled in. Never mellowed. She left her husband after only three years. He was nice. I never understood why she left him. She told me that once the shine wore off, there was nothing left but warts. What shine? Lust! As if sex is the most important thing in a relationship.

Derek claims men find Lita too stubborn. She's tough. A ball breaker. Aggressive. Outspoken. And won't back down. The opposite of everything Derek looks for in a woman. He met Lita when he came to Nanaimo to article. He says she always looked down on him because he was still articling and she'd been a lawyer for several years by then. Of course! He didn't go to law school right out of college like she did.

She had other faults, too, but it didn't take him long to discover them, and dump her. Besides, by then he was falling in love with me.

When it happened, Lita claimed she dumped him. Said she was sick of him always questioning where she went and who she called, and then he slapped her when she told him it was none of his business. Like it was somehow wrong for him to be interested in what was going on in her life. That was the last straw. Derek claimed he never slapped her and said no one likes to admit they've been dumped so she lied about it. Saying she lied is a bit harsh. I think she just didn't want to admit the truth. Derek started with her, but despite Lita being the pretty one, ended up picking me.

I got pregnant almost right away. Imagine that, in this day and age! I had quit taking The Pill because of weight gain. I didn't have a steady boyfriend and I thought I could avoid pregnancy by using condoms. That was before I started dating Derek! He said that sometimes he wanted me so bad he just couldn't stop long enough to put one on. Besides, it doesn't feel as good for the man, and he assured me he had been around enough to know what to do. No system of birth control is perfect.

We got married. I quit my job at the insurance agency and became a stay-at-home mom, even though we could've used the money when we bought this house. There wasn't much left from Derek's first wife's life insurance, so we had to take on a big mortgage, which of course comes with big payments. I went back on the pill then, because another baby was an expense we sure didn't need.

As soon as Jenny slept through the night, I got the cinnamon bun and muffin baker job at the Willow Point Café. I enjoy the cheerful bantering with the other ladies. Plus, it buys the groceries. At first it was only four hours a day, finishing before the cafe opened in the morning so I'd be back home when Jenny woke up. When she was old enough to get herself ready for school, I changed it to a full 8-hour shift, and left

Derek to get Jenny off to school. While I was baking and mothering, Lita concentrated on her career.

Lita is coming for dinner. I make a mental note to tell Derek when he comes in for lunch. I didn't mention it earlier because he was too focused on the bird feeder catastrophe, but he has to know these things in plenty of time so he can plan his day. I can't put it off.

I go to the window and call his name. He appears at the door of the garage. "Lunch is ready!"

He nods, then vanishes inside again. I turn the burner to low to keep the beans warm until he's ready to come in.

Jennifer skims into the kitchen, blonde curls framing her pixie face. She looks so much like her father it's heart-stopping. She holds up at the stove, grimaces at the fry pan, and screws up her mouth.

"Where's the French fries?"

"I don't have any frozen and didn't have time to make them from scratch today, honey."

"I don't want *that* stuff!"

"I know. I'll make you a sandwich."

"*Ffft*!" She expels her breath in a derisive snort just like her father does when he's annoyed. "Okay. I'll have it in here!" She disappears into the den with her tablet and in moments, the sound effects for some video game or other start up.

I paste two slices of Wonder Bread together with Skippy and strawberry jam, trim the crusts and cut the sandwich in thirds before putting it on a plate with a dill pickle and carrot sticks I know won't be eaten. I pour a glass of milk and deliver lunch to my beautiful daughter. She's so engrossed in the game on her tablet she doesn't look up. In a few minutes I'll look in and if she hasn't touched it yet, I'll remind her to eat before the bread gets dry.

I go and give the Yorkshire pudding batter another whisk before opening the oven door to pull the rack with the roasting pan forward.

The heat is unpleasant but the aroma makes up for it. I drizzle juices over the meat. It's going to be perfect!

I know it's too hot to have the oven on, but the weather's been changeable and I didn't want to chance a barbeque. Besides, if I made a simple steak, baked potato and salad dinner, Lita would pass most of her meat and half her potato to Derek and fill up on salad, going home as skinny as before. This way, there'll be roast vegetables, mashed potatoes, Yorkshires and gravy. I purposely didn't make a salad.

Dampness seeps into my T-shirt and my armpits feel uncomfortably wet. I wish I could wear a tank top or at least something with a lower neckline and short sleeves.

Living alone, cooking for one, Lita always looks underfed. I make a point of inviting her for dinner to make sure she doesn't starve. Although we text each other, these past couple of years Lita comes around less and less. I still invite her often but she's got so much going on she hasn't been here since spring.

Lita has had several romantic interests since her divorce but finds something wrong with every guy, so it's been ages since she brought someone with her. Rather than a date, her reason for declining invitations is as likely to be a seminar or golf tournament or some other event that's good for what she calls networking. She's only available today because I changed the invitation from Saturday to Sunday when she said she had a conflict.

The back door squawks open, signaling Derek has come in. The powder room door closes and I hear water running. In a few minutes, he comes into the kitchen.

"Christ, it's hot in here."

"If we'd finished that summer kitchen in the basement—"

"Or if you didn't make a roast in barbeque weather, heating up the whole damn house. I don't know what you're thinking sometimes." He snorts. "Smells good though. What is it?"

"Brisket. A big one, lots of leftovers, so you'll have nice sandwiches for days. It cooks slow, you know, low and slow. That's why I've started it already." I move toward him and stroke his shoulder, breathing deep of the male smell of him, enjoying the touch of his skin, wondering about my breath and whether we might have that kiss now.

But he goes past me to the fridge, opens the door and gets out a beer.

"I invited Lita for dinner tonight," I say. "Hope you don't mind. Cooking for one—"

"Yeah, yeah," he says. "I'll have my lunch on the patio. I don't know how you can stand it, cooped up in this inferno when it's so nice outside." He opens his beer, tosses the cap into the sink, and heads out through the patio doors.

I dish up, arrange everything on a tray, and join him on the patio. It'll be in the sun later, but now it's shaded. A welcome breeze, fragrant, cool, slides over me. I put the tray down on the table and lift my T-shirt to let the air cool my midriff, what Lita would call a muffin, before taking a chair across from him.

"No French fries?" he asks. He's not looking at me, though; he just takes his plate and starts in on his food.

"Sorry, I just didn't have time today. Breakfast was late, then I had to take Jennifer to swimming because you were working on your feeder. Then I had to shop and pick her up again, so I really just got home. I started late."

"I would have waited the extra fifteen minutes it would take to make fries," he says. He takes a long swallow of his beer, then loads his fork with cottage cheese and beans.

"I forgot I was out of frozen French fries. I'm sorry. I know I should've bought some today but I forgot my list at home and—"

"Out of potatoes too?"

"No. I, er, yeah I have potatoes but I didn't have time to make them from scratch and besides, I thought it was too close to dinner for such a big lunch."

"Don't you think you could've asked me about it?"

"I'm sorry."

"You should be," he says, and leans over his plate, shoveling his food down so fast I wonder if he even tastes it. Is that a scowl? I don't blame him for being annoyed. Lita's coming today, of all days, when he's so wrapped up with the broken feeder, and now no French fries. But when I invited Lita, I didn't know he'd be so busy.

"Honey, I know Lita's a bit, well, abrasive. But she's been a friend for so long. You know she can't cook! If I didn't invite her once in a while, she'd never have a decent meal."

"I'm pretty sure there's enough guys taking her out for dinner you don't have to worry about it," he says, his brows drawing together in a frown.

"Why do you think that? She hasn't brought a date or mentioned dating anyone for so long..."

"You don't really think she hasn't had a boyfriend since the last asshole she dragged around here, do you?"

"I thought he was all right."

"Pfft! Sure, if you don't mind someone with an IQ of fifty." He puts his fork down, gets to his feet, picks up his beer and heads back toward the garage. About halfway across the yard he turns and asks, "What time will she be here?"

"I told her drinks at four, dinner at five, since it's back to work for both of you tomorrow. Is that okay?"

"You didn't consult me on this, so it'll have to be."

"Maybe I should just tell her something's come up and she shouldn't come after all."

"Jesus, you're stupid, Carly."

"Sorry."

He pushes his hair off his forehead and whistles as he continues to the garage.

I hear the snick-snick-snick of pruning shears and realize Linda is just on the other side of the fence. I wonder how long she's been there. She's so close and Derek was so loud, I'm sure she heard Derek call me stupid. I feel like going up next to the fence to talk to her. Explain why Derek is grouchy today. But Derek stops in the doorway of the garage and looks back at me, so instead I put my empty plate on the tray, gather everything and return to the kitchen. I eat the rest of the beans including what Derek left on his plate while I stand at the sink. Waste not, want not, Mom always said.

I still haven't decided what to make for dessert. There are bathrooms to clean, end tables to polish, and time is passing.

Four

Lita

Nullah was still miffed about the whole Carly/Derek thing when he dropped me off. I told him not to spoil such a lovely day by pouting. He said he doesn't pout. So then he was pouting *and* pissed off. But Nullah doesn't stay mad long. I reminded him I would tell Carly and Derek about him, and to make peace, I agreed he would definitely go with me the next time.

I guess I'll do it, too, although I'm a hundred per cent sure it wouldn't go well. First thing Derek would do would be to ask him about his unusual name. Nullah would tell him it's a common Aboriginal boy's name in Australia, and although he's Māori, he was born and raised in New South Wales. He'd chuckle as he explained it means war club or digging stick. Not that Derek would give a shit whether Nullah was Māori or Aboriginal or Brazilian, he's brown, and Derek has never had anything good to say about people of color. I wouldn't put it past Derek to say something like *Carly, go dig up some nice fat earthworms to go along with War Club's rice.* But Derek wouldn't really be as big an asshole as all that. At least he probably wouldn't.

As I drive the highway heading for Cedar By The Sea, I indulge in a fantasy scenario of showing up this afternoon with Nullah. Imagine Derek's face! And if Nullah looked at Carly sideways? Oh my god, it would set off Thunder Brow for sure.

Carly is Rubenesque-beautiful. She doesn't realize it, though, and Derek's frequent comments about her weight don't help. In fact, it's as if she hides her body because she's embarrassed. Now that I think about it, maybe I *should* introduce them to Nullah. He says he loves zaftig women so it's kind of strange he ever asked me out, although really, what choice did he have after I climbed into his lap at Theresa's stag? (Nullah wasn't part of our party. He was just sitting with a few of his friends at a nearby table. In my defense, he smiled at me first. I also blame the shooters.)

Of course, he could've just dumped me. He didn't have to ask me out, there didn't have to be a second date, and now we're a couple, so my not being zaftig isn't a dealbreaker. Judging by how often he does it, he likes that he can easily pick me up, so maybe that was the initial attraction.

I'm the furthest thing from zaftig, like a stick next to Carly. I couldn't gain an ounce if I tried and my boobs hardly make a bump in a T-shirt. Nullah says any more than a mouthful is wasted. Still, I know he wouldn't be able to keep his eyes off Carly's double D's. Next time Derek comes out with a snotty comment about never taking Carly out on the boat because she makes the boat list to whatever side she happens to be on, I'll suggest he get a better boat. Maybe one like Nullah's. It would piss that asshole off royally and be good for Carly's self esteem besides, so it has everything to recommend it.

Five

Carly

Only a little after four, the door bell rings.

"I'll get it!" Derek yells from the second floor. He comes thundering down the stairs in a cloud of Acqua di Gio, crossing the foyer to arrive at the door ahead of me. He has showered, spiked up his hair and shaved for the second time today. Thankfully, he's ditched the jean cut offs. He looks trim and boyish in baggy plaid board shorts and a T-shirt that actually came with ripped-off sleeves so his biceps are exposed and even his armpit hair shows. It reads "NUKE THE GAY WHALES FOR JESUS". Lita points at his shirt and says, "You gotta decide on a cause, Derek." She chuckles but it sounds forced. I cringe, wondering if he's going to take it as an insult.

But Derek just says, "As with everything in life, I like to keep my options open."

Lita. Cool and unruffled as always, fresh faced and pretty even without make-up. She says hello and hands Derek a bottle of wine as she brushes past him and comes to give me a hug and an air kiss.

"Derek, why don't you take Lita outside and get her fixed up with a drink?" I suggest. "I'll join you when I can."

"Can't I help with something?" Lita asks. "At least I could have my drink here so we can visit while you work. We haven't seen each other in such a long time."

"No, it's all right, everything's done except for the dessert and it's a one-person job. I'll be done in a few minutes and then I'm going to run up and change out of these sweaty clothes. You go outside. We'll catch up at dinner."

"She's running behind. Disorganized as usual," Derek says, and hands me the wine.

"Carly disorganized? Never," she says, but she shrugs and follows Derek out into the backyard.

Watching from the kitchen window, I see that instead of getting her a drink, he's giving her his guided tour of the birdhouses, starting where the new feeder will go and working around the yard to the garage. I know from experience he's pointing out details, how nifty this one is, with the door that opens on the back for cleaning out at the end of the season, how that one has the perches under it for the fledglings, and on and on. They go through this every time she comes over, and still Lita pretends interest. She listens and even asks questions as he yammers on about birds.

Now they disappear around the corner to the front of the house as if they're heading down the trail to the water. I guess Derek wants to show her the new boat. I feel a rush of—what? Jealousy? Hurt feelings? Why am I left out? If they're going to go down to the dock, couldn't they wait until after dinner so I could go with them? We could take drinks down with us and enjoy watching the sunset over the water. Then I realize if we did that, it would be dark coming back up and the trail, especially the sections of rickety old steps Derek hasn't gotten around to fixing yet, is treacherous enough at the best of times. So I'm sure he is just thinking of safety.

I fold the whipped cream into the pudding mixture in the bowl, add the miniature marshmallows, then spatula everything into the lovely cut glass bowl my grandmother gave me. Three fresh mint leaves and a tiny viola flower from my garden for garnish, and it's into the fridge to set. It's supposed to be refrigerated for a couple of hours, but I was late making it. We won't be ready for dessert for at least an hour, which should be long enough.

I admit when I saw Lita, so cute and cool in her lacey sleeveless blouse, I felt a twinge of envy. I'm downright jealous of her flat stomach. No muffin there. Of course, she never had a baby and she's a runner. She's got time for that, with no kids and not much housework to look after. She's got good legs, too. There's no denying she looks good in that mid-thigh skirt. A nice outfit for a hot day.

I remind myself looking as good as Lita does hasn't gotten her a husband, or even a steady boyfriend. Beautiful, intelligent Lita, living alone in a two-bedroom townhouse while I live in this big house overlooking Dodd Narrows, with a beautiful daughter and a husband who still turns teenage girls' heads.

As I wash dirty utensils at the sink I see Lita return to the patio, a little red-faced and short of breath as if she must have run up the trail. She sinks to a lounger and swings her feet up. Knowing Lita, she would challenge Derek to a race and is so competitive she would practically kill herself to beat him. Derek appears moments later and fusses with pulling out the curtain surround before re-appearing at the bar. As he passes her a tall glass, he crouches on his haunches beside her.

Snatches of their conversation drift in through the open window. It sounds like she's telling him about an argument she had with someone, her voice rising and falling as she relates the story peppered with F-bombs. I cringe. Why does she always have to swear like that? It's so unladylike I'm surprised Derek never calls her on it. One of these days he just might. For now, I just breathe a sigh of relief that Jennifer isn't home to hear it, as she's having dinner at her friend's house.

I'm wiping the counter when Derek's loud laugh attracts my attention. He's still crouching beside Lita, smiling that heart-stopping big smile that crinkles his eyes, and says something too quietly for me to hear. He slides his hand between her thighs just as he moves so his back is to me, blocking my view.

My insides churn. I turn away, focusing on my task while my brain replays the caress. Was that really what it was? I only saw it for a split second, but it was too familiar. Maybe he did it without thinking, just being friendly because we've known each other for so long. But that's the wrong kind of friendly. Maybe I'm mistaken. Now I'm not sure it happened at all. If there was something going on between Derek and Lita I would know, wouldn't I?

"Of course you would, Carly," I mutter, and remind myself he broke up with her a decade ago because of all the things he didn't like about her and if anything she's gotten worse instead of better. I could hear all that swearing from here.

I go to the oven to check the Yorkshires. Damp hair sticks to my forehead. I haven't had a chance to change, much less shower. It's too late for a shower now, but the Yorkshires aren't brown yet so if I hurry, I have time to wash my pits and put on a fresh shirt before they have to come out of the oven. I dash upstairs, through the master suite, and into the ensuite bathroom, where I pull off my shirt and check the bruises. They've faded, but not enough. No sleeveless top today.

I wet a washcloth, and give my face, armpits and breasts under my bra a wipe. The cool damp cloth on my skin is so pleasant I do it a second time, then dry my pits and give them a swipe of deodorant. A clean shirt, a spritz of Red Door, and I'm good to go. When Lita and I were roommates, we called this a French bath. Arriving home after an all-night party with just a few minutes to get ready for work, we had French baths frequently. It seems like a lifetime ago.

Maybe I shouldn't have made a roast today, and maybe we should eat outside. But I've already set the table in my dining room with the china I've been collecting since I was a teenager, which I certainly wouldn't want out on the patio. And what about the centerpiece of dahlias from my garden I spent half an hour fixing? That would be ridiculous on the patio and besides, the patio table is too small.

But—Derek and Lita? It's impossible. Lita is exactly the type of woman Derek has never been interested in. They argue about everything. For what? Who cares if there were or were not five million Jews in Europe at the time of the Holocaust? Whether Ezekiel was visited by extraterrestrials and not angels, or was mentally ill or didn't even exist? Whether climate change is real and human-caused or part of a natural cycle? Whether Covid came from bats or escaped from a lab in China?

Lita disagrees with Derek on every subject. He hates being contradicted, as she very well knows, but she contradicts him anyway. I give myself another mental reminder that he wasn't interested in her back in the day and he surely couldn't be now. I tell myself to quit thinking about it and get a move on.

I cover my face with foundation. My skin's sweaty so it cakes and looks awful. I take the damp washcloth to it and wipe it off. I'll just have to go barefaced. I quickly stroke green on my eyelids, make a quick application of mascara and then dab my lips with Gypsy Rose Red, Derek's favorite shade. I run a brush through my hair, pull it back off my face and put a clip in it, then suck in my stomach and stand back to check my look in the mirror. I can't do anything about that muffin, but thanks to the heat in the kitchen, my face is flushed so the lack of foundation isn't critical and I certainly don't need blush.

I hurry back to the kitchen and discover Lita sitting at the peninsula with Derek nowhere to be seen. "What's up?" I ask. "Where's Derek?" I realize the tone of my voice is a little sharp. What I really want to ask her is why she encouraged Derek, her friend's husband—*my* husband!—to touch her like that. If he did.

"I guess he had something to do outside," she says, and she squirms on the stool as if feeling guilty.

Good! She *should* feel guilty.

"I came in to see if there really wasn't anything I could do to help," she continues, "but as usual, everything's under control. Unless you want me to—"

"Nope! Nothing for you to do."

The Yorkshires are finally just right, blackening slightly. I pull them out and dump them into the waiting napkin-lined basket. I take the roast out from under its tinfoil tent, carve it, and arrange the slices on a platter, adding a sprig of parsley and hand the platter to Lita.

"Okay, you want to do something? Take this in. I'll call Derek," I tell her, and go to the patio door to call him. He's in a chair, leaning with elbows on his knees, swirling the ice around in his drink.

"Everything's ready," I tell him, and go back inside.

As he comes into the kitchen, Derek says, "Didn't I tell you it's too hot to eat inside?"

Lita is standing in the doorway to the dining room and says, "Look at Carly, covered up from head to toe like it's winter. If she's not too hot, you and I can't complain." She produces an elastic from her skirt pocket and draws her hair up into a messy knot on top of her head. "Anyway, it's a treat, like going to a fine restaurant! Look how nice, even flowers. Are they all from your garden, Carly?"

"Umm, yes. Dahlias and snap dragons. I have my own baby's breath, too." I cast a quick glance at Derek but his expression is dark. He's been in a mood all day and it doesn't improve with Lita coming down on my side. I guess she'd be on his side if there really was something between them, so I take it as a good thing. It's Lita as usual. Nothing to worry about.

When she sticks up for me like she did just now I appreciate it, but it's not as if I'm incapable of defending myself. I just do it differently. Confronting him head on makes him angry, so it's best to ignore it, say nothing, or apologize and change the subject.

Lita couldn't put together a meal like this to save her soul. She doesn't even have a proper table because she says she prefers to perch on a stool at the island. No big deal because Kraft Dinner taxes her ability. The one and only time Derek and I went to her place for dinner, we took our plates to the stove and dished up spaghetti with the sauce already on it, right out of the pot. The empty Hunt's Thick and Zesty Mushroom Basil Sauce jar was still in the sink. Once when I invited her here, she asked if she could bring something. I asked her to contribute a salad. She brought it, all right, not in a bowl ready to be tossed with house made dressing as you might expect, but in a bag that hadn't been opened and Kraft dressings in bottles. She asked for my salad bowl and pointed out that there was a choice of two dressings, as if she was proud of it. I smile at the memory and wonder if she's thinking about it now.

When she tells Derek to get the wine, I realize she's not thinking back, but is in the moment, and has done something else that will irk him. Minutes ago she wanted to do something to help. Now she's giving Derek a task. I'm surprised when he doesn't argue.

I herd them into the dining room. Derek takes his customary place at the head of the table. I direct Lita to the far side and set the basket of perfect Yorkshires in front of Derek before taking the chair across from Lita.

"Lots of House Finches around this summer, hey, Carly?" Lita says. "They were buzzing around when we were out there. So pretty, with their rosy little heads!"

"They're anxious for the feeder to go back up," Derek explains.

"I thought you put it up this morning," I say.

"That was just to test the new hanger. My new feeder is quite a bit bigger than the old one. Needs a second coat of paint and I'm still trying to figure out a way to keep the squirrels out of it. I think I have an idea that will work. I might draft the plans and submit them to Modern Woodworking. They're always looking for projects to fill their magazine."

"You can draft plans that are good enough to submit to a magazine?" Lita asks.

"It's not difficult," Derek says, " not for me. I have a new CAD program I've been fooling around with. It's a really complicated program, not at all intuitive or user-friendly, but I've figured it out. Good for neural plasticity, learning different things."

"I'm learning to quilt," I say. "That must be good for—"

"It's hardly the same thing, Carly," Derek cuts me off. "Anyhow, I'll finish the feeder after work tomorrow. Hope I don't have to work too late. Don has been relying on me for so much lately, keeping me working such long hours I've barely had time to take the new boat out." He takes a thick slice of beef and as he passes the platter to Lita, tells her, "Don is the big boss—"

"Yeah, I know," Lita says.

Derek frowns at the interruption, but continues, "I've actually had to explain points of law to the other partners, even the guys who are more senior, so Don has his eye on me. I'll probably make partner and get a private office when the firm takes over the top floor. He's given me the nod for one of the corner offices."

"When's that happening?" Lita asks.

"Pretty soon."

"I thought Dennison Wealth Management had the whole top floor."

"Umm, yeah, that's right. They, er, do now," Derek replies.

"Are they moving? I hadn't heard that."

"Why would you hear about it? And I didn't say we were moving right away."

Before Lita can needle him any more, I ask, "So the new feeder is bigger?" I clench my teeth. More seeds equals more birds and more mess. I can't stop myself from saying, "I don't know why the birds have to fling bird seed everywhere. They waste more than they eat! I'm constantly cleaning up under that darn thing. And the weeds!"

"The Spotted Towhees clean up most of what's on the ground under it, if you'd just give them a chance," Derek says. "That's where they like to forage. Having the birds around is worth it. Pulling a few weeds isn't a big deal."

"I like the birds, too, but I know it makes a mess," Lita says. "Why don't you put it somewhere that weeds wouldn't matter, Derek, like at the back of the yard? Or around front where it's too rough to landscape anyway."

I catch a strange look between her and Derek.

"Yeah, a good place if you never want to see the birds," he scowls. "Defeats the purpose."

"Well, I thought the purpose was to help the birds. Plus, they don't live on the feeder. You've got birdhouses all over the yard. Unless the birds don't use them."

"No," I say, "Derek's right, pulling a few weeds isn't a big deal. I'm out there watering things anyway, and the birds are nice."

I take a bite of roast cauliflower. It's too soft and I regret putting it in the oven at the same time as the carrots and beets. No one else seems to notice, so I don't mention it. I tell Lita about Jennifer's latest parent-teacher interview, how the teacher said she has so many friends she is one of the most popular girls in her grade. A boy a grade ahead of her even took her to a movie! His mother drove them. Isn't that cute? From her expression, I gather Lita doesn't think so.

Before she can respond, Derek starts in about the boat and how he's working on fixing the steps down to the beach, the wharf, and maybe he'll build a boat house too.

"Say, I should take you gals out on the boat for a couple of hours sometime. You know I got it fitted with a commode, Lita, inside the cabin, so you don't have to use a bucket. Stainless steel. Such a thing of beauty it's sacrilege to shit in it. Looking at my wife's ass, maybe she won't fit through the cabin door, but you won't have any trouble, Lita."

Lita stiffens and frowns and I'm sure she's about to say something snotty so I quickly change the subject. "So, I thought I saw you going down to the boat, but you didn't?"

Lita gives Derek an odd look, then says, "No, we decided not to go that far or we wouldn't be back when dinner was ready."

"What were you guys talking about out on the patio? I heard you laughing."

"She was just telling me about something that happened at work," Derek says.

"Well, what happened at work that was so funny?"

Lita exhales loudly, frowns at Derek, then explains, "Just a run-in I had with that asshole, Bruce. I told you about him, remember? The one that's always such a pain in the ass."

"Isn't that the guy who's single?"

"Yeah, divorced. No surprise there."

I might remind her that I could say the same about her. I don't, of course. I press on. "Maybe he'd ask you out if you didn't always snipe at him."

"Honey, he's the last person on earth I'd go out with." She studies her plate, then adds, "If not last, then second last." She gives Derek another cold look.

"But you must be lonely," I continue. "You said he's good looking. And he has a good job. Why not give him a chance?"

"I'm not lonely, Carly, but even if I was, I wouldn't go out with him. There isn't a single thing about him that I like. Other than he's pleasant to look at, I guess. Like a lot of pretty people, once you get to know him, you don't notice his good looks anymore." Another sideways glance at Derek.

"But what's wrong with him?"

"Well, he's a smarmy ass kisser for starters. And he has no idea how to deal with people, especially the secretaries. If he was in charge, everyone in the steno pool would walk out."

"What do you mean, walk out? They'd get fired if they did that, wouldn't they? Don't those gals want to keep their jobs?"

"Of course they want to keep their jobs. I meant figuratively. Still, they don't have to put up with his bullshit. He treats them like slaves. He's that guy in the office who always has a last-minute emergency. He's not senior enough to have his own secretary, but is so full of himself he thinks his job, any job, should go to the head of the queue. I've let him put one of his jobs ahead of mine a few times, but it's chronic. I finally had enough, took him aside and quietly told him to fuck the hell off. What does he do? Goes crying to the claims manager. I get called in shortly after. There he sits, shit-eating grin on his face, expecting me to be reprimanded. Instead, he has his ass handed to him and I got my own office and my own assistant."

"Oh!"

"Yeah. It's tiny and a long way from a corner office, you know, but much better than being out in the cubicle farm." She looks at Derek again before continuing, "And now we're really at odds. You wouldn't believe the looks he gives me."

Going by the dark expression on Derek's face, he hasn't missed the jab and I have a pretty good idea of the looks Lita gets from the guy in her office.

I say, "But that's just work. Maybe he's different away from the office."

"Sure. And maybe pigs can fly."

"Lita, let's face it, you're not getting any younger. You shouldn't be so picky! You're going to end up spending the rest of your life alone."

She spears a caramelized carrot and pops it in her mouth, chewing and swallowing. Then she leans toward me and says, "There are worse things than being alone."

What could be worse than being alone? I study her pretty face and notice new lines at the corners of her eyes and bracketing her lips. Pretty, popular Lita, now she's this pathetic, lonely person, and she doesn't even realize she's her own worst enemy. If it wasn't for our shared past, we'd have nothing in common. I have no funny work stories to share and no one would have any interest in anything I do. She acts as if it's a mortal sin we only have one car and Derek takes it to work. It's not like I need it; I have plenty to do around here without running into town all the time, and on weekends Derek lets me use the car to shop and take Jennifer where she needs to go.

For the first time, I realize how judgmental she is. It's sad, but we're drifting apart. Maybe it's time I accepted it. I hear myself sigh, and say, "Lita Muldoon, you'll never change."

She smiles as if it's a compliment. Scooping up the gravy boat, I add the dregs to the teaspoonful she had put on her small mound of mashed potatoes and go out to refill it. When I come back, Derek reaches for the gravy. I hand him the gravy boat and say, "There's a nice pistachio and pineapple mousse for dessert. It's light, so you don't need to save room." I scoop up roasted vegetables and put a good spoonful on everyone's plate before sitting down.

Derek opened the wine Lita brought and poured each of us a glass before dinner. Now he takes the bottle out of the ice bucket and tops up our glasses. Raising his, he looks at Lita and says, "Here's to beautiful women."

Lita gets an odd look on her face, then says, "Here's to the feeder."

Well! Couldn't she be gracious and acknowledge the compliment? She's looking at me. For a moment I think she's going to say something else but then Derek drains his glass and leaves the table, coming back with a second bottle. He pours himself another glass, but Lita and I haven't finished ours, so he puts the bottle in the ice bucket.

Lita sits there sipping wine and watching us eat. I see her spear a small beet, cut it in half and stir it around in the gravy before eating it, but that's it. I might as well not have given her more vegetables.

When Derek is finished, I suggest dessert. Lita, no surprise, declines. Derek says it's too soon, takes the wine bucket and his glass into the living room and tells us to come with him. I open the doors to the deck and suggest we sit outside. I haven't seen the schedule for cruise ships but it's the season for the Seattle to Alaska run so there might be some passing. Lita sits in the only chair at the far end of the deck instead of at the table with me. Derek hops up on the rail beside Lita. I have a millisecond's mind picture of him toppling off.

After a few minutes of idle conversation, it's obvious we have nothing more to talk about. Lita says she has to go but will help cleaning up the kitchen first. Derek tells her she doesn't need to bother because I prefer to do it in the morning. Really? That's the first I've heard of that! He knows I always make sure everything's tidy before I go to bed. I'll do it as soon as she leaves.

A quick goodbye and she's gone.

Derek watches out the living room window and I go into the kitchen to start cleaning up. There isn't much mess because I always keep on top of it as I cook. It's mostly just putting all the leftovers away. I'm bent over digging through the bin of Tupperware, when I hear him come into the kitchen. Ice clatters as he slams the bucket down on the peninsula. I straighten and turn to face him.

"She left in a fuckin' big hurry," he snarls. "You had to remind her she's getting old?"

My heart thumps.

He's not here for dessert.

Six

Lita

As expected, I'm barely in the door before Carly shunts me off outside with Derek like she can't bear to be alone with me even for ten minutes even though we haven't seen each other for months. I wouldn't say anything critical of him even if she let me help in the kitchen and he was elsewhere. I mean, not when I just got there. But after a few glasses of wine, if he would ever bugger off and leave the two of us to talk? Maybe. Probably.

I promise myself that today I won't say anything to rock the boat. I won't criticize him even in the off chance he should leave us alone. I won't argue with the asshole. I won't suggest he could do something to make Carly's life less miserable such as "babysit" so she could have a night out with the girls once in a while, or even, at a minimum, do some yard work. He doesn't even run the damn lawnmower! If that's not the husband's job, I don't know what is. Imagine how long her days are, getting up at three to go to that café, be home again in time to get Jennifer off to school, and keep that house and yard looking like a page out of Better Homes and Gardens.

This last is a problem of her own making, though. She's obsessive about household tasks. When she told me she irons Derek's shirts and then hangs them exactly three inches apart, I laughed. Believe it or not, it wasn't a joke. When I realized that, I told her she really should lighten up. She said that's how Derek wants it, because if shirts hang too close together they get wrinkled. He's on his way up, clothes make the man, he has to look good, yada yada. Besides, although I can't imagine why, she likes doing things for him. He's so grouchy it's beyond me why she keeps him around. It's not because he has a big dick or even that he knows how to use it. But I won't say anything. Nothing! Nada! Zip! My lips are sealed.

Of course, he wants to give me a tour of his birdhouses. It's too good to be true, but there are new ones. They're nice, although the outdoor ones aren't as fancy as those inside that no live bird will ever be near, and I admit he's talented with his fancy little saws and miniature nails and so on. I go along with it, ooo-ing and ahh-ing when appropriate. It's not totally disingenuous because I really do like the birds and the little houses are attractive, but I could give a shit whether the joins are rabbeted or butted.

Then he says, "Hey, let's go down to the wharf. I want to show you my new boat."

"Oh, umm, I don't think we have time before dinner," I tell him, "let's go after instead so Carly can come with us."

"Come on," he coaxes. "It'll only take a few minutes. Carly doesn't like it and anyway, she'll still be fussing around in the kitchen when we get back. I really want you to see the new boat." I guess he senses my hesitation, because he adds, "I've mostly fixed the stairs."

I'm really not interested but it's better than sitting on the patio listening to him pat himself on the back. I follow him around to the front of the house.

This area, at least, Carly is content to leave alone. It's the way nature made it, beautiful in its way, rugged; rocky and overgrown with salal, huckleberry and ferns. The house is perched at the top of what you might call a cliff except it's not a complete drop off, just a steep decline. From the yard, you're looking out at the tops of sixty- or a hundred-foot firs. A previous owner hacked enough trees and bush away to make a trail down to the water, with sections of actual wooden stairs. I've been down a few times and it's nice when you get to the wharf, but not nice enough to warrant climbing back up minutes before dinner. It's taxing for me and really difficult for Carly, so she might not want to go anyway. We start off down the first set of stairs and head into the shady part of the trail.

When we come to the second staircase, Derek turns so suddenly I nearly bump into him, and his arms go around me. He's looking down at me with a weird, creepy expression like he's going to kiss me.

"What are you doing?" I hiss.

"Come on, Lita."

I try to push away from him, but he clasps my arms. "Let go of me!" I demand. He drops his hands to his sides. I turn and hurry back up to the patio, arriving at the pergola while he's still some distance behind me. I hear clattering noises coming from the kitchen; Carly is still busy in there, so if I go in now, she'll likely just shoo me back out. But I think she needs to hear about what just happened, so I go to the door.

Then I rethink it. Is this the right time? Is there ever a right time? Maybe me shutting him down like that is enough. I go back to the pergola and settle on one of the lounges, turn my face up to the sun, and close my eyes. When Derek comes back up, I'll ignore him.

Soon I hear Derek fussing around the back of the pergola. He's unsnapping the curtains, pulling them around so the whole area is shaded, whistling as he works.

I don't open my eyes when he comes up beside me. Is he going to comment on what happened on the trail? I think about what to say if he does.

He goes to the little fridge in the bar cabinet and I hear the pop-fizz sound of a bottle being opened, then ice clinking in a glass. "Here you go," he says, "your favorite brand of peach cider."

I open my eyes now and look up to take the drink.

He goes back to the counter, puts ice in glass and half fills it with scotch. Instead of taking the other lounger or a chair, he comes to squat on his haunches at my side and I think, *here it comes*. But he says nothing, just squats there staring up at me.

After an uncomfortable moment, I launch into a tale from the office. He laughs harder than the story warrants.

"That guy fancies you, Lita," he says. "Who can blame him?" He's wearing that smarmy grin of his. The next thing I know, he sets his glass on the table, slides his hand between my thighs and murmurs, "Lita…"

I utter a hiss and jump up, hurrying into the family room in time to see Carly disappear down the hall, apparently on her way upstairs. I head into the kitchen to perch on a stool at the peninsula, wondering what on earth is going on in that man's head. Did I do something to give him the idea I'd welcome that? More likely it's just stepping up the intimidation from verbal to physical. Should I tell Carly?

I'm still mulling it over when Carly comes down, a cloud of perfume preceding her. She's put on that deep red lipstick she always wears and changed her shirt, although she hasn't put on something cooler, just switched into another oversized long-sleeved shirt, already damp in the pits.

I should tell her now. But she gives me such an angry look I'm taken aback. What's that about? Is she really that unhappy about me coming into the kitchen when she told me to wait outside?

She asks, "What are you doing in here?"

"I, um," I gulp and take a breath. I guess coming inside before being summoned is a crime. This isn't like Carly. Somehow I can't tell her, not when she's already hostile. "I just thought maybe there was something I could do."

"Nope," she snaps, "there's nothing for you to do."

Well! I wish I could leave right now. But that would be childish.

She opens the oven door, shrinks back at the blast of heat, pulls out a pan of Yorkshire puddings that would make the buffet at the Chemainus Dinner Theatre proud and dumps them into a waiting cloth-lined basket. She lifts the tinfoil tent off the platter of sliced meat, hands it to me and says, "You wanted something to do? Here. Take this into the dining room."

I'm just setting it on the table when I hear Derek say, "Jesus, it's hot in here. I told you I wanted to eat outside."

"But there's too much…"

"At least we should dish up in here and take our plates outside."

"But my table—"

From his tone, I take it there's been something going on between them today. Maybe Carly's bad mood is because of that, and not anything I did. I turn and go back to the doorway and tell Derek, "It's hot outside too, and this is a real treat, like going to a fine restaurant. Look how nice, even flowers. And Carly is covered up from head to toe. If she's not too warm, you and I can't complain." He frowns at me like he's going to argue. I frown right back and with a lift of my chin, say, "Why don't you get the wine?"

He presses his lips together but goes to the fridge while Carly busies herself scooping roasted vegetables from a pan into a bowl. I wait until she comes into the dining room and directs us to our seats. I'm on one side, Derek at the head, and Carly sits across from me, closest to the kitchen.

The food is delicious as always, even though it's really more like winter comfort food than anything for a hot summer day, and I would have much preferred a salad. Conversation goes along okay. Jennifer is a superstar swimmer, her teachers all think she's the best ever and more Jennifer this and that. Carly tells me she had a date with a boy, as if that's something to be proud of given she's not even ten years old. She looks a little deflated. She must've read the disapproval on my face and doesn't say anything more. Thankfully Derek starts in on his boat again before I'm expected to come up with a comment.

Of course, Derek could never just talk about his boat, he has to brag. He even brags about the portable commode and manages to work in an insult about the size of Carly's ass. I'm torn between telling him about Nullah's boat, which has two bathrooms with heads, not com-modes, or remind him he couldn't keep his paws off Carly's ass even in company when they started dating, when Carly changes the subject by asking what we were talking about earlier, on the patio. I look at Derek, who glances at me but otherwise ignores the question, so I tell her about Bruce. Of course in her view, I should suck up to him in hopes he might condescend to date me. She thinks I'm lonely? Maybe this would be a good time to tell her I'm too busy to be lonely, I have other friends besides her, and I have Nullah.

But then she makes a comment about me getting older and being so picky I'm going to be alone all my life. The way she says it makes it sound like a fate worse than death. I have to bite my tongue. Does she really think it's better to be a marriage slave like she is? Has she for-gotten all we used to talk about and dream about when we were room-mates? It's true she always said she wanted a husband and a kid, but not until she had done some living. She got Derek and Jennifer before she had a chance. Finally I say, "There are worse things than being alone, Carly."

She gives her head a shake and says something about me never changing as if sticking on the path to what I always wanted is a bad thing. Then she jumps to her feet, picks up the gravy boat and empties it onto my plate so now everything is swimming in it, and leaves.

As soon as her back is turned, Derek looks up, grins, and I feel his foot twining behind mine, lifting it. I pull my feet back under my chair. He winks as if my not saying anything condones it. Like it's our naughty secret, which I suppose it is. When Carly returns with the gravy boat, she hands it to Derek and scoops more vegetables onto my plate. This is what Carly does: she feeds people as if they couldn't help themselves. She should've had more kids.

"You don't need to feed me, Carly," I tell her.

"Someone does," she replies. "Eat up! I think you're skinnier since the last time I saw you."

"I don't think so. My clothes all fit the same as always."

Derek pulls the Riesling out of the ice bucket, tops up our glasses, and says, "Here's to beautiful women."

I'm totally creeped out by the look he gives me as he says it. I suppose I should respond. Can I just say something generic like *I'll drink to that*? No. I force a smile and say, "Here's to The Feeder." Although meant as a compliment to Carly, I realize it came out as kind of a snipe. I should have said "Here's to our beautiful hostess".

Judging by their puzzled expressions, Derek and Carly think it's an odd toast. They're right. I study the vegetables swimming in gravy on my plate. Derek drains his glass, goes to the fridge, and comes back with another bottle.

I was already quite full before Carly gave me those veggies. I was raised to eat everything on my plate, but that doesn't count if someone else dishes up for you, so I toy with my food, watch and sip wine while they clean off their plates. Carly offers dessert. I decline.

Derek says, "Not now, Carly. Let our food settle. Let's move to someplace more comfortable." He stands, picks up his glass and the wine bucket, and heads into the living room. We follow.

The living room! The enormity of the privilege isn't lost on me. Bad enough we're leaving footprints in her carefully-vacuumed carpet, I'm afraid my glass might leave a ring on the shiny table and mentally curse Carly's trendy new stemless glasses.

Thankfully, we don't have to stay here. Carly asks, "Should we sit out on the deck?" She goes to draw the drapes and opens the doors giving onto the deck. Cooling, ocean-scented air sweeps in. "There should be some cruise ships going by."

"Yes, lets!" I hurry out and take the chair at the far end. No chairs near enough for the asshole to play footsies, and no problem putting my glass down on the table here.

There are bird houses here, of course, and some I don't think I've seen before. I'm not going to mention it, though, because I don't need more mansplaining about the dangers of too much glue in a joint. I already know it's a rookie mistake, one which naturally Derek has never made.

Carly sits at the table, but Derek hops up on the railing beside me. Carly makes an odd comment, like he should be careful. It's a long way down, for sure, but he's not a child. Much as I wouldn't mind if he toppled over and was never seen again, there's no chance of that. It's difficult maintaining a friendship with someone when you dislike their partner enough to wish something awful would happen to them.

Derek starts talking about the new boat again. He can afford it because he's doing so well, having just snagged a hefty retainer from some drug company. Hard work, all those extra hours, pay off, he assures me.

Carly mentions quilting again and says she would like to upgrade her sewing machine. Derek says there's nothing wrong with the one she has and wonders what good quilts are when they have duvets. With the money he's making she sure as hell doesn't have to make her own bedding. He goes on to tell me about his latest workout routine and how his personal trainer says he's the poster boy for office workers everywhere. And it's a good thing he's strong and fit because working on the steps down to the beach and fixing up the old wharf is taking some real manpower besides construction skills. The previous owners did a shit job of it. It's astonishing how people put up with such crap materials and poor workmanship.

I stifle a yawn.

After a reasonable amount of time has passed, I say, "I know it's early but I've got an appointment first thing tomorrow and I have a lot to do yet tonight, so how about we clean up the kitchen now?"

"Carly will clean up the kitchen in the morning," Derek says. "Have another glass of wine."

"No, Derek, I've had plenty, and I have to drive. Thanks for everything, though." I get up and head out through the living room to the foyer. Condensation rings be damned, I set my half-full wine glass on the table there and retrieve my purse from the hallstand. I say good-night, give Carly a hug, and escape out the door.

As soon as the door closes behind me, I feel a wave of relief and ask myself if it was just Derek that made me feel uncomfortable all evening. Every time I see them, he's kind of flirty in a creepy way, but tonight was over the top. I wonder if he really wants that kind of relationship with me or if it's just intimidation. We were over and done a decade ago, after all, and didn't part amicably. I'm torn, thinking I should tell Carly he made a pass at me but not wanting to hurt her. If I told her, would he back off or would she side with him and blame me, ending our friendship?

And then there's Carly herself. She seems different. I've noticed it before, but it was more pronounced tonight. What is it? Stress? Tension? I can't put my finger on it. Did she even smile once?

She used to be more fun. We wouldn't have been friends if she'd always had such a stick up her ass. Once she finished raving about her daughter, with 'Derek said the teacher said' and 'Derek said the swim coach said', she hardly spoke more than half a dozen sentences. I don't sew, but I wouldn't have minded hearing more about quilting and less about Derek Fucking Wilton! At one point I even felt like saying *I came to visit Carly, not you, Derek*. But I had promised myself I'd hobble my lip about him, and I did. But that look she gave me when she came down and saw I wasn't on the patio where I was supposed to be! What was that about?

We've been friends for years, but as some poet once said, times change and we with time. I know I told Nullah he would come with me the next time, but I don't want another boring, awkward evening like this one, ever. Maybe I should tell her what Derek's been up to, even if it's the end of Lita and Carly. Maybe it's time.

I call Nullah from my car to see if I can come over for a hot tub. He agrees, and half an hour later, we're submersed.

Hot tub is a misnomer, because Nullah turns the temperature down during the warm months so it's more of a slightly warm tub. Very pleasant. The property is rural, totally private (no suits required), and away from city lights so you can actually see the stars. I lean my head back on the edge of the tub and let my body go weightless, watching the stars start to pop into view in the twilight as the water slides seductively over my skin.

"So," Nullah says, "you're back early. I wasn't expecting you tonight at all. I barely had time to get those Swedish twins out of my bed."

I sit up and try to squirt water out of my hand into his face, a little trick I learned from him. He can nail you with a stream of water right in the face from across the tub, but I'm still practicing. He grins at my feeble effort.

I describe the miserable visit, stuck listening to Derek pat himself on the back. He seems to think me struggling to keep from yawning or the fact the news of my promotion barely registered with them, taking a back seat to their obvious disapproval of my life, is humorous.

"I didn't know you were so lonely, babe," he says. "You should've told me, instead of sending me home all the time."

"I seem to remember you were at my place this morning. And most mornings for these past couple of months."

"So why didn't you tell them that? It would shut them up."

"I almost did. But then Carly came out with a comment about how I'm not getting any younger, I was in no mood for that! I had to bite my tongue or I'd've given her a blast, but I know she means well and doesn't deserve it. Still, I've never seen her so disapproving. So judgmental! Every time she looked at me it was like she was studying a bug and thinking of squashing it."

"Are you sure you're not imagining it?"

"I'm sure." Then I tell him about Derek making that very unwelcome pass at me on the trail and then sliding his hand up my skirt when I was on the lounger.

His happy face disappears. He utters a kind of growl like something from his old rugby team pre-game haka, and says, "I'll beat the snot out of the little fuck."

"See? I knew you wouldn't like them. But anyway, you won't get a chance. And besides, if I made him sound like a pansy, he's not. I guess you'd say he's in touch with his feminine side, fussy about his clothes and like that, but he's only a little shorter than you are and he works out, too. In fact, to hear him talk, he's the poster boy for office workers the world over."

"Oh, I see," he says, and slides across the tub so he's between my legs and his hands are on the edge of the tub, one on each side of my shoulders. "You think I would only beat on him if he was a pansy, as you put it? You seem to have a low opinion of me, babe." He tries to look offended but the twinkle in his eye and his tiny grin give him away.

I slide my hand down his washboard stomach and discover something that makes me grin, too.

Seven

Carly

I hear the back door open and then close, then voices. I'm expecting Jennifer, but not Derek. What is he doing home from work so early? I sit up as the two of them come out of the back hall and into the family room.

Jennifer breezes through the room with barely a glance in my direction. Derek has a bouquet of flowers and comes to stand beside me.

"I brought you these," he says as he hands me the bouquet. "I hope they make you feel better."

"Thank you," I murmur. "I'm sorry, Derek, I was just resting for a minute. I... I... um, I just didn't get much done today. I haven't got anything ready. I didn't expect you home so early." I start to get to my feet.

"I'm home early because I decided to pick Jennifer up from school. Here," Derek says, reaching for the flowers, "let me take those. I'll go put them in water. You stay put."

I gladly sink back against the cushions while he takes the flowers into the kitchen. I hear him whistling as he opens and closes cupboard doors, then calls out, "Where do you keep the vases?"

"Under the sink," I reply. There's shuffling noises and the clatter of glass; the water runs, and in a few minutes Derek is back in the family room. He puts the flowers on the coffee table and sits on the couch next to me, taking my hand.

Jennifer comes back downstairs and I hear the pantry door open. "There's no cookies!" she shouts. "You were supposed to make cookies today!"

"Your mother isn't feeling well, Jennifer," Derek calls back. "You know she got hurt when she fell."

"But I'm hungry!"

"Get something out of the fridge. Cheese or something. There must be something else for your snack."

After grumbling and rummaging in the fridge, Jennifer leaves the kitchen and heads up the stairs, leaving Derek next to me on the couch. He squeezes my hand and says, "About last night. I'm sorry, honey. I had too much to drink. I realize it now. I lost control. I just couldn't help it."

I take a deep breath. I know I'm supposed to tell him it's okay, as I always do. That's what he expects. I don't want him to get mad again but I can't quite bring myself to say it.

"I apologized. Don't you have anything to say?"

"Umm... I'm sorry. I, er. I know you had a bad day."

"That's right. But you don't know the half of it. Honey, I feel so bad! I'm going to tell you something... I haven't wanted to tell you this, she's your best friend and everything, but now I have to tell you." He heaves a great sigh, releases my hand and sits up straighter. "You know Lita has always had a thing for me?"

"You mean *before*. She had a thing for you *before*."

"Well, she's never given up."

"What do you mean?"

"She keeps after me, honey! I've told her so many times I'm not interested because I love you so much and I would never, er, do *anything*, do what she wants, with her! But you know even before we were married, after you and I got together, she kept after me." He fixes me with an intense look. "Yesterday was the worst."

"I know you had a bad day. The bird thing," I nod, remembering the bird feeder and then no French fries. I should have realized how stressed he was when he started drinking scotch even before he went up to shower.

"The feeder, not 'the bird thing,'" he says. "But it was more than that." He sighs, gives his head a little shake and clicks his tongue. "She made a pass at me."

"What? I can't believe it!"

"Well, believe it. When we started down to the dock so she could see my new boat—where you wouldn't be able to see us—she pressed herself up against me and tried to kiss me. I pushed her away! She wouldn't let go! Finally I broke away and went to the patio. When she came and sat down, I'd had time to compose myself and I went on as if nothing had happened. I know how much the dinner meant to you. How much effort you had put into it! So I didn't want to spoil it for you by confronting her. I made myself a drink. She wanted a peach cider, so I gave her one."

"But I saw her come up. She was ahead of you. She was on the patio before you were."

"Yeah. When I pushed her away, she ran past me." He looks off over my shoulder for a second, then takes a breath and hurries on. "I couldn't put up with that, honey! You know I couldn't."

"So why did you... Why did you put your hand on her thigh?"

"Oh, you saw that? See! I didn't tell you about that because then I'd have to explain and I knew it would hurt you! I was trying to be gentle with her, to make her understand, but in a nice way, so as not to ruin the mood, not with the beautiful dinner you had worked on all day. I told her that she isn't going to get with me again because I'm still so much in love with you. I just put my hand on her knee and she squirmed. Deliberately, to make my hand slide up! Oh, god! I hate to say it but I had to get rude with her. She didn't take it well. Did you see all the nasty looks she gave me for the rest of the evening?"

I manage a slight nod. I had noticed the nasty looks. Now I know the reason.

"And then she was playing footsies with me under the table. I ignored it. What could I do? But when she finally left, I was angry about the whole debacle. I thought it was your fault. I thought, Carly must see what she does. Why does she keep inviting that awful woman?"

"No... I..."

"I know it's not your fault, honey. It was my fault, totally my fault. But I had too much to drink. It was just the booze. My emotions got the better of me. I thought you might blame me. That would ruin our relationship. What if you didn't believe it was her, all her? What if you thought I had somehow invited her advances? You might leave me and I don't know what I'd do if I lost you. I lost control. I'm so sorry, honey." He pulls me into his arms. "It won't happen again, I promise. Forgive me?"

I squeeze my eyes shut, begin to relax into the manly warmth of him, and murmur, "yes."

He smothers my face with kisses, then gets to his feet. "Good. You stay here. I'll go get changed, and then I'll mow the lawn."

"But your feeder..."

"I know I was going to finish that up, but I don't want you having to mow the lawn until you're feeling better. I thought we could go to the Simon House for dinner tonight. So when you're up to it, why don't you go and put on some nice clothes."

He gets up, then looks down at me and smiles. "By the way, you can sleep in tomorrow. Your job at the café? You don't ever have to go back there. When I called and made your excuses this morning, I told them you quit."

What? I'm blindsided. I manage to stammer out, "But I... I like it! I don't want to quit."

"It's a nuisance, you getting out of bed so early every morning. Too much of a nuisance. You know it always wakes me."

"But it seems like you sleep through."

"I don't say anything, but I'm awake. And it's a damn nuisance having to deal with Jennifer. When I'm really busy at work, I'd like to go in earlier and instead I have to hang around here until she's ready."

"I'm sorry. You should've told me. I could change to a shift later in the day."

"No. I'm doing great now, you know that. I'm going to make partner soon. Look, I had no trouble getting that loan for the boat, did I? We don't need the money. You've got plenty to do here, looking after Jennifer and the house and the husband that loves you."

"But I should at least give notice."

"No. I don't want you going there again, having to work with those ball-busting high school dropouts. You're not like them. You know you don't fit in there. They're beneath you. I told them you wouldn't be coming back. And honey? Speaking of ball-busters, I don't think you should be friends with Lita any longer. Stay away from her. No more invitations, okay?"

I nod slowly. My head is spinning. I'm out of a job on top of the news about Lita? The early morning hours of the job weren't the greatest, but the ladies I worked with weren't ball-busters. Sweet, shy Ariana, a student working on her PhD, always ready with a smile. Georgia close to celebrating her fiftieth wedding anniversary, taking care of her ailing husband. She should be retired but they need the money, always cheerful despite her troubles. It was a hectic time, getting everything ready for the café to open. We worked hard but we worked well together and had fun doing it. Now I won't be going there anymore?

And Lita? How could she pretend to be my friend when all the while she was trying to get Derek away from me? How could I have been oblivious to it? Most of the time it seems she really doesn't like him. It must be an act, so I won't suspect anything. Back then, she was too proud to admit he dumped her and not the other way around. Still, we've been friends for so long. If nothing has happened, it's not too late. I'll tell her to leave him alone, and put this behind us.

"Maybe I should talk to Lita—"

"No!" he snaps. His eyes turn black and intense as they do when he's getting angry. "You think I don't realize how she poisons you against me? You stay away from her."

It's true that every chance she gets, she criticizes him. I whisper, "Okay."

The tension leaves his shoulders and his frown relaxes. "Good," he says. "Now I'll go and do the lawn."

I breathe a sigh of relief as he turns and walks away.

Simon House. Haven't been there in years. Not since my elbow was dislocated.

Eight

Lita

After that dinner, I decided my friendship with Carly was over. Nullah's been harping at me about giving her another chance, something one on one such as coffee at Starbuck's. It bugs me, mostly because I know he's the one who's being adult about this. So I texted her. About six times. Finally, I called.

Although she's virtually a stay-at-home mother of one child who's in school all day, Carly is remarkably unavailable, too busy all this week and into the next. I can't believe the excuses she's come up with. I'm not so obtuse I don't get the message: I am not important enough for her to postpone her daily floor washing, furniture polishing, weed pulling or shirt ironing and would you believe it's been months since she washed the top of the cabinets?

Nullah points out that she has no vehicle, and says, "Maybe you should offer to pick her up."

"You don't think I thought of that? She is obviously just as done with me as I am with her," I insist. "Now she doesn't even respond to my texts. Fuck her and her asshole husband!"

"And you said you weren't into threesomes."

"Piss off," I mutter. At this moment his little grin and the twinkle in his eye is annoying rather than endearing.

He lets out a little snort, then says, "How about this: don't give her a chance to say no. Get a couple of donuts or something and show up on her doorstep one of these mornings."

"One of these mornings that I'm not working?"

"You're flexible. You're not chained to your desk."

I consider it for a moment, then ask, "Why do you give a shit?"

"Why?" He drains his coffee, then signals the server and asks for the bill before answering. "I know you have other friends, but none that you've had for so long. Since high school. You're lucky and I envy that."

"You've got friends. Lots of them."

"Sure, but my old mates, the ones from school, I left behind when I moved here. You two have history."

"Well, people grow apart, you know. If you'd stayed in Queensland, you might not even like your old mates anymore."

The server brings the bill. Nullah pays and we walk out holding hands, through the parking lot to his truck. As we're driving away, I say, "You know, I think part of the reason I've had it with Carly is that I've lost all respect for her. I couldn't believe it when they started dating. I told her I thought he has narcissistic personality disorder. That's incurable! She just blew it off. Made some comment about me thinking I'm a psychologist. Didn't seem to care that the main reason for us splitting was him being too controlling, or that he even slapped me."

"He slapped you?"

"Only once. But it was hard and it hurt. That was enough. Why would she let herself in for that? And now it's as if that man controls every part of her life. I don't know why she doesn't stand up for herself."

"Low self esteem. She should join one of my self defense classes. Knowing how to defend yourself does great things for a person's positive self-image and confidence."

"You've never suggested me joining."

He barks a laugh and says, "You know, as small as you are, it would be good for you to learn a few things. But you don't have to join a class unless you really want to. I'll give you a few pointers, one on one." He manages to make a leer look cute, then continues, "I've never noticed you had a shortage of confidence, though, babe." He reaches across the console, takes my hand and draws it to settle on his thigh with his big paw resting on top of it. "You didn't put up with him for long, did you?"

"Too long. A few months. Long enough for him to think he somehow had the right, or even the duty, to slap me over something so trivial I don't even remember what it was. As if I was a child to be punished. I realized it wasn't going to get better. I wasn't in love with him, and honestly, I'd begun to realize I didn't even like him much, so I would have broken up with him anyway. She never should have gone out with him in the first place but it's not too late to get rid of him and I just don't understand why she doesn't."

"No way of knowing. She has a kid now, maybe she stays because of that. Or finances. But I do think you should give her another chance."

"I'll think about it," I agree. "Oh. By the way, your friend Craig is an investment advisor at Dennison Wealth Management, right?"

"Uh, yeah. Why?"

"Are they moving?"

"Not that I've heard. Again, why?"

"Nothing important. It was just, I was thinking about something Derek said at dinner. He said his firm is taking over the top floor of the building they're in. You know, where Craig's company is. I told him I hadn't heard Dennison was moving. You should've seen his face. I think he realized he was caught in a lie. He said he didn't say it was right away, just that it was soon. I should've told him I know one of the partners at Dennison and he hadn't said anything about it. Instead, I let him get away with it. As usual, I let his self-aggrandizing and lying go unchallenged. I guess I thought maybe Craig just hadn't mentioned it."

"That would surprise me. I had drinks with him not that long ago. Something like that takes planning. I'm sure he would've been talking about it."

"I think so too."

"I'll call him and find out, if you want."

"Yes, please."

Nullah pilots the truck to the curb in front of my office and says, "See you tonight? We can throw that salmon on the barbie."

"Sounds good. See you tonight." I lean across and give him a kiss before hopping out onto the sidewalk.

It'll be interesting to hear what Nullah's friend Craig says about relocating their office, but I'll bet dimes to donuts Derek was just shooting his mouth off, full of shit as usual. If I'm going to have any kind of relationship with Carly going forward, letting Derek get away with this kind of bullshit has to end. No more Ms. Nice. I will make it a point to fact check him in real time, right on my phone while he sits there watching me do it so Carly can see what a lying, pompous ass he is. I won't wear a skirt so he can't put his hand up it. If he tries anything else, ever, I will call him out on it right when it happens. Although, maybe the course of least resistance would be to make sure Nullah always goes with me. I wonder what would happen if Derek made fun of Nullah's name. Maybe Nullah would punch him. I doubt it and I wouldn't want him to, it's just something I do in my mind. I'm sure the visit would be chilly, at best.

But first, I have to see Carly. I suppose I need to apologize but although I wrack my brain, I can't think of anything I did that was offensive enough to make her so mad she wouldn't even answer my call. I'll ask her, and whatever it was, I'm sure we can put it behind us.

WEDNESDAY. IT'S 10:00 a.m. and I'm on Carly's doorstep. It's a school day and teacher's professional development days are always either Mondays or Fridays so unless she's sick, Jennifer won't be at home. The family SUV is not in the driveway, there's no room to park in the garage so it can't be there, meaning Derek isn't home either. On my way here I went to the Tim Horton's drive through and got half a dozen muffins. Box in hand, I ring the doorbell.

There's movement inside and I think Carly is coming to open the door, when I hear her ask, "Who is it?"

"It's me, Lita," I reply. I know she can see me through the peephole so her question is irritating. It's all quiet inside and the door remains shut. After a moment, louder this time, I say, "Carly? It's me, Lita."

"Lita? How come you're not at work?"

"I had a couple of errands out of the office so I thought I'd stop by. I brought these," I say, and hold up the Tim Horton's box so she can see it.

"Well, you should've texted first. You can't come in! I'm sick."

"Oh no!" I say. "Well, I'll stand back. I'll just say hello and leave you these."

"No! I don't need anything. I'm going back to bed now."

"Carly? Carly!" No response. I stand on the porch staring at the peephole, examining my feelings about what just happened and wondering what to do. I guess I'm pissed off, and I then tell myself I shouldn't be, since she is just being super careful not to take a chance on infecting me with whatever she has. With the pandemic still fresh in everyone's minds whenever someone coughs, everyone immediately wonders if Covid-19 is back. But social distancing only means staying two yards apart. It doesn't mean she couldn't open the door.

After a moment I decide to leave the muffins on the bench by the door. An apology for whatever I did that she didn't like. Peace offering. Then go to my car and drive back to my office. At least it's a pleasant day for a drive in the country.

Eight

Carly

I'm doing the ironing, humming as the iron huffs out clouds of steam. Even though we're well past summer and there's a nice cool breeze from the open window, it's hot work. There's no one around, so I push my sleeves up.

The bruise covers my forearm from wrist to elbow. It's quite pretty, really, dark blue, purple, green turning yellow. I know the black socks always go on the left, brown in the middle, and navy on the right so he doesn't make the mistake of wearing the navy ones with the black suit. I screwed up. I can't blame him for being mad.

Despite the heat, I'm enjoying the scent of fresh laundry. This is the last shirt, then it's on to underwear. Boxers can't be folded properly if they aren't ironed, something Lita would never understand. She never even ironed her husband's shirts. She thought that being Permapress, they didn't need it. She doesn't know how to look after a man. She hasn't figured out that if you look after your man, he will look after you. It's a two-way street. She's had so many guys in her life and not one has stuck around, whereas Derek and I just passed our eleventh anniversary. He has stayed with me even though I'm far from perfect. He knows I'm trying, and I'm learning.

Here I am, thinking about Lita again. I guess it's not surprising my thoughts turn to her so often. I've long since lost touch with other friends; Lita's the only one who is still a friend. *Was* still a friend. We were best friends since high school and really only split after Derek and

I got married. It wasn't a total split at first, of course, just sort of a cooling off. Growing apart. I realize now Derek encouraged distancing because she wouldn't quit making passes at him. I'm still astonished I was oblivious to it all those years. I have half a mind to call her up and demand an apology. Or at least let her know he told me so she doesn't think she's gotten away with it.

I haven't had contact with Lita since she came for dinner back in August and went after Derek so brazenly. There was just that one time. Jennifer found the Tim Horton's box of muffins on our doorstep and brought it in. It was sitting on the counter, open and with a couple of muffins eaten, when Derek came home. When I told him it was from Lita, he flipped out even though I assured him I had sent her away without even opening the door.

I don't blame him for getting mad, because I had agreed to quit being friends with her. He was still very upset about the shameless passes she had made at him and another reminder of Lita trying to worm her way back into our lives understandably sent him over the edge. I told him I had put her off when she phoned. I showed him the texts, proof I hadn't arranged to meet with her, but he didn't believe me because I could have deleted the incriminating ones. I told him I didn't even know it was possible to do that. I suppose I wouldn't have believed that, either. Anyway, I have a new phone now, and a new number, but it's just for us, our family, so Derek and Jennifer can get a hold of me if they need to.

Even though I miss seeing the people from the café, I have to admit since I quit my job there, I'm a lot less stressed, probably because I'm not as tired and have more time to take care of things around here. I know I was also spending too much time on the internet looking up recipes, in addition to the YouTube and Facebook timesucks. When he doesn't take it with him, Derek's laptop is in his study and the door is always locked, so I'm not tempted to waste time like that. I won't be giving my new phone number to Lita, so I'm freed up to take better care of everything.

I miss my old phone, though. The new one isn't really new, just an old dinosaur of a flip phone Derek had years ago that he had re-activated. All you can do is phone with it. Well, you can text, but it's pretty tough since there are three letters on each number. I went down the beach trail to where he threw my iPhone and found it, but it was smashed.

With Lita out of our lives Derek has gone back to being the loving husband he was when we first married. And the sex! Even on the lounge chair on the patio and standing up against the railing on the stairs on the beach trail! At first I was reluctant to go along with it. What if someone saw us? But with such a steep drop-off to the beach no one can come near our house on that side, and with all the trees and bushes on the other three sides it's all very private. Who could see us? I'm sure the neighbors could've heard him, though! Four or five 'oh gods' just like in the beginning! I feel myself blushing at the thought. Thankful-ly it's too cold outside now. And this is really new: he often wants sex before we get out of bed in the morning. He has even kissed me before I've brushed my teeth.

Right now, I have to finish up the laundry and then make sure the house is ship shape, because Derek has invited a big wig for dinner tonight. He is Mr. Ewan Finnegan, CEO of a multi-national with its head office in Toronto. Some of the other lawyers invited him too, but he accepted Derek's invitation, so this is a real feather in his cap. If he gets this done, lands this retainer, the corner office is a done deal for sure. It would be a good time for me to bring up the idea of me getting my own car again. So it's important for Mr. Finnegan to be impressed.

Derek dug out one of my old blouses from the back of the closet and said he wants me to wear it tonight. That really surprised me be-cause I quit wearing it years ago when he told me I looked like a hooker, showing all that cleavage. It does have a really low-cut neckline. I didn't get rid of it, though, because I've always loved it; it's filmy and delicate, with embroidery and tiny seed pearls on the sleeves and around the neck. I always felt like a princess when I put it on. For a while when no one was home, I would put it on just for an hour or so. Childish, I know, wasting time playing dress-up like that. I haven't done that for so long I'd almost forgotten it and I'm surprised Derek knew it was in the closet. And it's an even bigger surprise that he wants me to wear it. He said he wants to show off his beautiful wife! Imagine! Him calling me beautiful!

Thank god I tried the blouse on. I managed to get it done up but it was snug around the middle, so I carefully let the darts out and moved the buttons over as far as they could go. It's supposed to be looser, more flowing, but that's the best I can do. I'll put it on last thing just before Mr. Finnegan is due, because the bell-shaped sleeves are so long they almost reach my knuckles and are constantly getting in the way. I don't know who designs these things. Maybe Derek's right and I just have disproportionately short arms.

I wish I had something interesting to talk about when Mr. Finnegan comes, but I've never been a good conversationalist. I'm worried I'll say something stupid and embarrass Derek. Derek said the men will have plenty to discuss and me just sitting quiet and looking pretty is more than enough. Me, beautiful, and now pretty!

Derek's been gone most of the day. He picked Jennifer up from school and they went to the mall to get her some new clothes. She's grown so much all her pants are too short. Then he'll drop her off at her friend's birthday party. It's a sleep-over, so I don't need to worry about her. We adults will have the dinner table to ourselves. It's been such a long time since anyone but Lita has come for dinner or even a visit, and a now it's man, an important one, from Toronto. It's looking like it will be a most excellent day.

I hang up the last shirt, measuring to make sure it's three inches from the next one, and bring the stack of boxer shorts to the ironing board. It won't take long to get them put away.

I'm making Chicken Kiev, risotto and asparagus spears with hollandaise sauce. Cherries jubilee for dessert. At this time of year I could only get canned cherries, which isn't the greatest, and I couldn't get pitted ones, but I've got the pits all removed and everything else is organized too: butter sticks in the freezer; parsley minced; chicken breasts teased open, pounded just a bit and waiting in the fridge; eggs separated. I've even set the table, cutlery perfectly spaced and napkins ironed and folded into perfect fans. I'll have plenty of time before I have to start cooking to get myself ready.

Since Derek phoned to tell me he was coming, I've been wondering what Mr. Finnegan looks like. Ewan Finnegan sounds like an Irish name. I visualize him with piercing blue eyes, dark hair greying at the temples, tall, trim and handsome. I hope he has a nice lilting Irish accent, although I suppose I'm letting my imagination run away with me because it's likely his family has been in Canada for generations.

I've been fantasizing about having sex with Mr. Finnegan. I feel a little jolt of guilt mixed with desire as I think about it again, and imagine Mr. Finnegan drawing me into his arms in a gentle, loving way. He takes his time and is oh, so gentle. No squeezing my neck or biting my nipples, and I know he'll make sure I'm satisfied. Afterwards, he asks if it's all right for him just to hold me.

I feel a stirring deep inside. I hope he'll like me.

Nine

Lita

So today is the big day. It's official. I'm moving in with Nullah. I'm filled with apprehension at this big step, both wanting it and fearing it will ruin what's been a really nice relationship so far. We've been dating for less than six months. I worry it's too soon because we don't really know each other. We're both still so careful. So polite. Nullah still goes on fart walks. I thought we should wait at least until he felt comfortable enough just to let 'em rip. Maybe it's a case of be careful what you wish for.

He pointed out he's never heard me fart, either. He said he's not really surprised, though, because women don't fart; instead, they hold onto them. They end up stuffed with farts, the farts travel up the spine into the brain and that's why women get shitty ideas. *That is not original and also sexist,* I told him. *I wouldn't have expected it coming from you!* He said it's not sexist, it's just a fact. I said at least women only have the occasional shitty idea, only when they've been saving their farts. Men get shitty ideas constantly even though they have no excuse because they don't save their farts. Also not a sexist comment because it's just a fact. He said I'm awfully damned opinionated for a Sheila. I threw my slipper at him.

He should be back any minute. I've got most of my personal stuff packed and waiting in the entryway. I'm not moving my furniture or anything, not yet. We haven't decided what to do with my place, whether we should keep it as is so we can stay in town if we've been drinking and don't want to cab it all the way back out to Nullah's, or if I should rent it. I thought about putting it up for sale, but that's definitely premature.

I haven't lived with anyone since I was married, so seven or so years on my own. It's going to be quite an adjustment, getting used to living in someone else's place. Nullah says from now on it's not someone else's place, it's our place. We discussed a prenup, but talking is as far as we got. He doesn't seem concerned, surprising, given how much he stands to lose if we split up after even just one year. He's not a stupid man. He knows the risks. He's willing to take them.

It'll be a big adjustment for Nullah, too, since he's never lived with anyone, despite having had three what I would call long-term relationships: one for three years, which is as long as I stuck it out with my husband, and two of a year or so. So our relationship histories are pretty similar. I'm not sure if that bodes well for our future together and it's the reason I won't make a decision about selling my condo for a while. It'll be my fall-back position. Nullah understands that and is good with it. Obviously, if the wheels fall off our relationship, he doesn't want to be stuck with me even short-term just because I have nowhere else to live, any more than I want to be stuck with him for the same reason. I guess we're a couple of rolling stones. Question is, can we roll together?

I hear a vehicle and go into the kitchen to look out the window. Nullah's truck pulls up to the curb and backs into the driveway. I go to the door and greet him with a quick kiss.

"Is that it?" he asks as he surveys the pile of boxes.

"Yup. For today, anyway," I tell him. "I'll need to unpack a few boxes and bring them back so I can get the rest of the stuff out of the freezer."

"Maybe all those frozen dinners can stay here."

"What? Don't be silly."

"Kidding. We should pick up a couple of pizzas on the way home."

Home? This is my home! But looking around, seeing the entry closet empty and my espresso machine missing from the kitchen counter, it already looks less like it.

"Excellent plan. I'll order them now." I get my phone, go to the Pizza Hut website and place the order. Then we pack the rest of the boxes, my laptop, a few more garments on hangars and a garbage bag full of shoes into the truck.

WE'RE AT THE ISLAND in Nullah's kitchen, pizzas in boxes open in front of us. I've eaten half the small feta and spinach one while Nullah has nearly finished the large meat lovers with pepperoni and extra cheese. Just looking at it, thick and shining with greasy melted cheese, makes my stomach contract. I'd be up all night if I ate anything that rich this late in the day, but he has a cast iron constitution.

"I don't have much left to unpack," I tell him between mouthfuls. "Thanks for making room in your closet and in your dresser drawers, but there still isn't enough space for everything."

"I'll clear those shelves in the guest room. That should make enough room for another couple hundred shoes. And we'll get another dresser."

"I don't have a hundred pairs of shoes."

"You've got nearly that many here and you still have some at the condo." He shakes his head. "What is it with women and shoes?"

"Like you don't have dozens. Anyway, for dressers. I might as well bring one of mine."

"Makes sense," he agrees as he picks up another piece of pizza and engulfs about a third of it.

I watch in amazement as he manages to chew that big mouthful without even smacking his lips. Then I say, "Impressive! You didn't even have to tamp that in."

"What?"

I shake my head. "Nothing. I was just thinking, it's too bad we went ahead with this move the one weekend the big boss man was in town."

"It works out. He met with lawyers this morning and spent the rest of the day making surprise visits at the clubs up island. We'll spend tomorrow with him. He wants to do some fishing, so we'll take him out on the boat first thing."

"He wants to fish? Or you do?"

He grins and admits, "Both."

"It's kind of cold to be out on the boat."

"We won't be out for long. Dress warm, or stay below and read if you want. We'll hit the Dinghy Dock for lunch. Come back here in the afternoon. We'll get a fire going in the firepit. Some of the others are bringing stuff, salads, appies and so on. We'll throw steaks on the barbie. A fresh fish if we're lucky. In any case, we'll entertain him all day. Tonight, he's had an invitation from someone else for dinner."

"Oh? I didn't realize he knew other people in town."

"It's more of a business dinner. Some lawyer he met today. You know we're looking for a local lawyer, right? Someone conversant with leases and franchising, anything else that might come up. Probably won't find one here, it'll likely end up being someone in Vancouver, but it would be a lot more convenient to have someone here in town. Our Toronto lawyers made some enquiries and gave us a short list. One of the guys from a firm we're looking at invited him."

"You didn't want to meet with him too?"

"Well, I was helping a friend move."

"I'm sorry."

"Don't be. If he likes the guy, there'll be plenty of time for me to meet him."

"I guess." I drain my glass and toy with another slice of pizza, then decide against eating it. "I wonder if it's someone I know."

"You'll have to ask him. I didn't catch the name. He's going to brief me later so I didn't pay a lot of attention." He takes another bite and washes it down with the last of his beer. "He asked why I hadn't suggested you."

"And you told him I only do insurance defence work."

"Yup. Just as well. I don't like mixing business with pleasure." He slides off his stool and goes to the fridge to get another beer.

I hold out my glass and say, "A refill while you're up, please."

"Are you sure?" he asks. "I know you don't have much left to unpack but I thought you wanted to finish tonight so you'd have empty boxes for the rest of your stuff."

"What's that got to do with me having another glass of wine?"

"Well, you know how horny you always get when you've had a few. I'm afraid you'll cast your eyes on me and get sidetracked." He gives his crotch a quick suggestive tug, then grins and winks.

"Oh yeah? So you'd rather I spent the rest of the evening in a bad mood unpacking and putting things away instead of cheerfully fucking your brains out?"

"Point taken," he says. He takes my glass, fills it, and comes back to take his stool beside me. He puts my glass down in front of me and touches my neck, then runs his finger along the neckline of my shirt before slipping his hand down to stroke my nipple. An electric current courses through me.

"Mmmmm," he growls. "Drink up! It's past my bed time."

I grab his wrist and pull his hand away. "I think I'd like a soak in the hot tub first."

"No. Bed first. Hot tub after."

Ten

Carly

Headlights shine through the dining room window as a car pulls into the driveway. "He's here," I call out, and go to stand beside the stairs as Derek comes into the foyer.

He checks his look in the mirror of the hallstand, finger-combs his hair, smooths his shirt, then turns to me and asks, "How do I look?"

"Fine."

The doorbell rings. As usual, Derek waits a few seconds so as not to appear over-anxious, the pulls the door open. "Hey," he says, "welcome! Come in. Any trouble finding the place? I know it's tricky in the dark."

"Passed the driveway once, but that's it," he replies, and smiles at both of us.

I'm a little taken aback at how different he looks compared to how I imagined him. He's taller than Lita but definitely not as tall as me, and very muscular like the fighters in the MMA matches Derek watches on Pay Per View. He's dressed in jeans and his jacket has a logo that's a silhouette of someone holding barbells. His hair is very short and almost completely white, with a substantial bald spot. His eyes are as piercing and blue as I thought they would be, though, and he has a nice smile. Best of all, his voice is pleasant and he has an Irish accent. It's subtle, but definitely there. He hands a bottle of wine to Derek, and Callebaut truffles in a shiny box, to me.

"Thanks for this," Derek says with a lift of the bottle. "Leave your shoes on. Let me take your jacket, though. How about a drink before dinner?"

"Um, sure, that would be nice." He slips his jacket off to reveal he's wearing a polo shirt with the same logo as his jacket.

Derek takes his jacket and hands it to me with the wine. "Right this way," he says, and is halfway down the hall to the family room where the liquor cabinet is before he realizes Mr. Finnegan has stayed with me.

"Here," Mr. Finnegan says, "I'll do that." He takes his jacket from me and hangs it on the hallstand as he says, "And this lovely lady must be your good wife."

"Carly..." I mumble as I nod.

Derek says, "Carly, this is Mr. Finnegan."

"Pleased to meet you," I say.

He reaches out as if to shake hands but since I have a bottle of wine in one hand and the chocolates in the other and also because people have mostly quit shaking hands since the pandemic, he thinks better of it, puts his hands together and gives a slight bow. He says, "Pleased to meet you, Carly. And please, call me Finn."

We make eye contact. For a second I believe I am the only person in his world. As if I'm important. I think I understand why he is successful. "Finn," I agree. I glance over Finn's shoulder and see Derek watching, his expression dark. I shrink back.

"Let's get that drink," Derek says. "She has things to do in the kitchen." He waits until Finn's back is to him and gives me frown and a jerk of his head to direct me into the kitchen, then leads Finn into the family room.

I have everything set to go but there are things that can't be done ahead, and anyway, Derek told me earlier that he wanted private time with Mr. Finnegan before dinner. Making the Hollandaise, shallow frying the chicken and finishing the risotto and asparagus takes nearly half an hour. I hear the men's voices, although not clearly enough to catch more than a few words, or make out what they're talking about. It sounds like they're having a serious, productive, discussion. Here's hoping!

I open the wine and set it in the ice bucket on the table, light the candles, and call the men in. Derek takes his usual seat at the head of the table. Rather than having him across from me, I've set Finn's plate on my left at the foot of the table. I sit on the side nearest the kitchen.

"This looks terrific, Carly," Finn says, and gives me that engaging smile as he picks up the tongs and helps himself to a Chicken Kiev before passing me the plate. I watch covertly as he spears his chicken, elated when melted butter squirts out just as it's supposed to. He slices off a piece, puts it in his mouth, and gives a groan of approval. I'm almost giddy with relief.

Dinner goes along very nicely. I eat quietly while Finn and Derek chat about hockey, politics, the economy, other man stuff. When Finn has eaten all his asparagus, without thinking, I serve him more.

"Thank you," he says, "you know, my mum used to do that, serve more food like that."

"She always does that—feeds people whether they want it or not—you don't have to eat it," Derek tells him.

"No, it's great. It just brought back a very fond memory," Finn says. He looks into my eyes and says, "I mean it. Thank you."

I blush, give Derek a victorious smile and say, "I hope you like Cherries Jubilee. That's what I'm making for dessert."

"I've never had it but I know what it is. I like cherries and anything with ice cream gets my vote. Carly, you really put yourself out," Finn says as he cuts off another bite of chicken. "This chicken practically melts in your mouth. You didn't have to go to all this trouble."

"She wanted to," Derek tells him.

"Yes," I agree, encouraged by Finn's addressing me directly. "My Mom always said, cook your man happy. It's good to have a chance to make something other than meat and potatoes, or Derek's favorite bean dish that our daughter says looks as though it's already been eaten once."

"Sounds appetizing," Finn chuckles.

I chuckle with him. I chance a look at Derek and realize he's not only not chuckling with us, but doesn't look amused. I get a sinking feeling. I'm talking too much, and I shouldn't have said anything about the beans. Fortunately, his dark look passes quickly, and he says, "Well, like I said, you don't have to eat it all. If I ate everything she put on my plate I'd be as fat as..." He stops mid-sentence and glares at me.

Finn is watching us with an unreadable expression; after a second, he says, "Well, I sure appreciate it. I don't think I've ever had anything this good."

High praise! I feel as if I must be glowing.

Derek takes the wine bottle out of the bucket and tops up Finn's glass and his own, then says, "So, about the retainer, Finn. You didn't tell me... When should I send you a contract?"

"Contract? Well, I'd like to see a proposal first. You got the invitation to submit a bid proposal, correct?"

"Yes, but I thought... I just assumed since we're here now, you had chosen me, um, er, us, my firm."

Finn puts down his knife and fork and wipes his mouth on his napkin. "Oh, I'm sorry if I mislead you, Derek. I haven't made a decision. I thought you understood that."

A flicker of shock crosses Derek's face. He clears his throat and says, "I umm. Yeah, of course. I just meant, when will everyone be submitting bids? Did I say contract? I mis-spoke. I meant proposal."

"And of course," Finn continues, "I want to see everyone's CV's."

"I thought you were only looking for one lawyer."

"Hmmm, probably only need one for now, anyway, but I like to get experience with a few lawyers to see who's the best fit. And I won't be formally choosing one for a while at least. If it turns out you and I, or more importantly, you, me, my partner and our Toronto lawyers, are the most simpatico, well, then..." He shrugs, picks up the hollandaise bowl and spoons sauce over his risotto, then loads his fork with it.

"I see," Derek says. "You really don't have to go through all that. I can assure you I am the most knowledgeable. Other guys might have more experience, but don't forget, I'm a member of the bar in three U.S. states, too, so if you have any thoughts of expanding down south, I can take care of that."

"We have considered opening in the U.S."

"Food for thought, right?"

Finn shrugs and agrees. "Food for thought."

"Ask anyone, I have a high degree of legal scholarship, academic talent, analytical and writing abilities, because when I came here, I had to sit eight—fucking eight!—challenge exams before I could even article. Think of it! I aced them all."

"Impressive," Finn says.

"So anyhow," Derek continues, "I've had way more education than the Canadian guys. I know more about their laws than they do. I've even had to school the senior guys in our firm." Derek picks up his glass and downs half of it at a go. "Believe me. I'm your guy."

Finn's forehead creases in a frown for a second, then he smiles at Derek, shrugs and says, "Well, then, uh, that'll make for an easy decision." He turns his attention to finishing his dinner.

I breathe a sigh of relief, stand and take his plate.

"I'm done, too," Derek says, pushing his plate, still mounded with risotto, toward me.

I ask, "Should I serve dessert now?"

"Not now. Let's go in the other room, where it's more comfortable," Derek says, and gets to his feet. "Or, we can take a breather outside and I'll show you the beach access I've been working on. I got it fixed up so now I keep my boat right there."

"But it's dark out," I say.

"You ever heard of flashlights?" Derek snaps.

Finn glances at his watch and says, "Actually, I wouldn't mind dessert now if that would be all right. It's getting late, it's been a long day and I have an early morning. As pleasant as this has been, I'm afraid I'm going to have to cut the evening short."

"Of course it's all right," Derek says, and sinks back to his chair, deflated.

"It'll take me a few minutes to get the dessert ready. You can show him the top part from the deck," I suggest.

"Sounds good," Finn agrees. The two men get up and head across the foyer to the living room.

I stack my plate on Finn's and take all three to the kitchen, scrape and deposit them in the dishwasher. While the cherries and sauce are heating, I scoop a well-packed ball of ice cream into each dish.

"Dessert is served," I sing out as I bring the desserts into the dining room. I stand next to Finn's seat, Kirschwasser and a lighter at the ready.

Finn slides into his chair. When I've poured a nice quantity of liqueur on the mound of ice cream and sauce, I click the lighter and put the flame close to the dish.

The liqueur, at first reluctant to ignite, suddenly bursts into flame with a *whoosh*! Flames lick my hand and in the blink of an eye, my sleeve is on fire. I drop the lighter and jump back with a cry.

Finn reacts instantly; he leaps up, knocking his chair over in the process, grabs my arm, and wraps his napkin around it. He holds it tight and pats it all over, making sure the flames are smothered. In a moment, he pulls it away and confirms the fire's out.

"Oh my god," he cries, "are you burned? Sit down!" Holding my upper arms he gently but firmly guides me back to my chair and once I'm settled, pushes the sleeve up to my elbow to examine my hand and forearm. Thank god it's not my bruised arm. He takes my hand in his and turns it over, making small sounds of concern.

I manage to choke out, "I'm okay. Thank you." I'm shocked, of course, but gather my wits and say, "Really, thanks to you, I'm all right.

My blouse is ruined but it's an old one, and your dessert is still okay." I muster a smile.

"She's fine," Derek says, and fills his glass again, "but I'm going to keep my distance when she lights mine, just in case." He laughs that awful barking laugh that tells me he's drunk, and pushes his plate well away from in front of him.

"Okay. Sorry 'bout the chair," Finn says, setting it upright and sitting down again.

I roll the ruined sleeve back so it's out of the way and ignite the liqueur on the other two desserts without incident.

"Carly, get some liqueur glasses. We'll drink this stuff instead of burning it," Derek barks, brandishing the Kirschwasser bottle.

Shots of Kirschwasser is the last thing Derek needs and certainly not something I want, but I get two glasses out of the china cabinet and put them in front of Derek.

"Not for me, thanks," Finn says, "I've had plenty to drink and I have to drive."

"Naww, never! A Mick turning down a drink? What's that saying, an Irishman is never drunk as long as he can hold onto one blade of grass and keep from falling off the earth? I'm sure you can still hold onto the grass! Drink up!" Derek guffaws and fills both glasses, passing one to Finn.

I draw a quick breath. I wish he hadn't started drinking as soon as he came home after dropping Jennifer off. First he starts to slur, and now he says that? Did Finn take it as a joke or was he offended? I can't tell from his expression.

He says, "You and Carly go ahead."

Derek shoots his Kirschwasser and refills his glass, then says, "So. What is it you're doing tomorrow that you have to get up early for?"

"My partner is taking me fishing."

"Why didn't you say you wanted to go fishing?" Derek demands. "I could've taken you fishing."

"I haven't seen my partner since I flew in this morning, so we need a chance to talk, anyway."

"I'd like to meet your partner. I could take you both out on my boat. Too bad it's dark or I'd take you down 'n' show it to you. It's a twenty-one footer. Plenty of room for all of us."

"Hmm, maybe next time," Finn agrees. "Say, maybe you know his girlfriend. She's a lawyer."

"Oh yeah?"

"Yeah. Her name's Lita—"

"Lita, Lita, Lita!" Derek interrupts, expelling his breath in a whoosh. "Not many of those around. Lita Muldoon. Yeah, I know her." His eyes narrow as he says, "You're not using her for your corporate work, are you?"

"Um, no."

"Good! Because it's not her area of expertise."

"That's right. I understand she's an in-house lawyer for an insurance company."

"Right," he smirks, "in-house is a good gig for a lawyer who couldn't make it in private practice."

"I met her when I was here a few months ago. I found her very impressive and I'm sorry she's already taken," Finn says.

"She only does insurance defence work. She'd be no good to you," Derek tells him.

At the sharp tone of Derek's voice, a frown flickers across Finn's face. Then he looks at me and says, "This was delicious. Thank you. The whole dinner was very nice. But I'm going to take my leave now."

"But—" Derek objects.

Finn is already up and is heading for the foyer. Derek gets up and follows. I fall in behind.

"Thanks again," Finn says.

"When will I hear something?" Derek asks.

"I really don't know for sure. I have to run it by my partner. We're not in a big hurry because we have lawyers in Toronto, of course. I want them to have input into the decision. They've already vetted your firm and put it on the short list, which is why I wanted to meet with you."

"Good, then. Will I hear something before Christmas? After Christmas? When?"

"Probably not until after Christmas. Thanks again." He opens the door, steps out and pulls it closed behind him.

I'm a little worried about his hasty departure, and hope Derek is too drunk to think anything of it. I go back into the dining room, blow out the candles and start clearing dessert things.

Derek comes in, takes his seat and refills his liqueur glass. He drinks it and pours another. He's frowning.

"He seems nice," I say. "I think he really likes you." I pick up the candelabra and reach for the peppermill. He grabs my wrist, twisting so hard I drop the candelabra and crumble to my knees beside his chair.

"Oww! Derek, what...?"

He releases my arm and gives his half-eaten dessert a shove that sends it flying off the table, the bowl smashing into pieces on the wall. "He seems nice," he mimics me in a falsetto voice. "I suppose you think that went well?"

"I...I...yes I think it did! I think he liked you!"

"You think he liked me? I'm sure he liked *you*, especially after you nearly set him on fire!"

He gets up and takes me by the hair, pulling me to my feet, kicking chairs out of the way as he drags me around to the other side of the table. "Now look what you made me do! Clean up this mess!"

I struggle against tears as I fall to my knees to begin picking up the pieces of the bowl. I'm scooping ice cream onto the biggest piece when he hovers over me, takes my hair again and pushes my face down into the mess. I feel a sharp pain on my cheek just under my eye. He jerks my head back and forth, rubbing my face in the sticky mess. When he releases me I sit back on my haunches, uttering a sob.

"Clean it up!" he shrieks. Then he has my hair again and slams my face into the wall. I feel an odd numbness in my nose and hear a ringing sort of sound. Everything seems far away. I realize he's yelling at me.

"And there you sat with your tits on full display like a fuckin' whore, sucking up every word out of his mouth. And that fuckin' sticky mess of rice! He had to put sauce on it to even choke it down! And there you were, making sure he got a good look at your tits! You want to fuck him, don't you!"

"N...no! No, I—"

"And then you're so fuckin' clumsy you set yourself on fire? It's just a lucky fuckin' thing you didn't start *him* on fire! What a *fucking* disaster! You think he's going to give me the retainer after you fucked everything up like this?"

"I'm sorry! I'm sorry!"

"You should be! You know what? I've had about enough of you! You're not fit to be my wife. You're not fit to be anyone's wife! No one else would put up with you. And you sure as hell aren't fit to be Jennifer's mother. All you ever were was a brood sow and I don't need you for that anymore. I'll kick you out and you'll never see Jennifer again. Better yet, one of these days we'll go for a boat ride, and you won't come back."

I look over my shoulder and realize he's taken a step or two back. He lifts his fist and I shrink away, throwing up my arms to protect my face. But the blow never comes. Instead he kicks me. I sprawl backward. In a moment, I hear the back door slam shut and then the car starts. He's going somewhere, driving, as drunk as he is. I hope he doesn't kill someone. But at least he'll be gone for a while.

I get to my hands and knees, then sit back on my haunches again, sobbing. There is blood on the wall where my face hit it. I gingerly touch my cheek where it's stinging. My fingers come away red. My nose feels numb and blood streams from it. I wonder if it's broken.

The blouse is very revealing but he wanted me to wear it. Maybe it was clumsy of me to let my sleeve catch fire but accidents happen. It's only been two weeks since I screwed up his socks. Two weeks since he apologized profusely, swore he only did it because he lost control of his emotions, and vowed he would never do anything to hurt me again.

I wipe my face on my sleeve. Now there's a smear of blood on the blouse along with the burn. He's never cut me before and he's usually careful not to mark me where it shows. This is an escalation. It doesn't matter how hard I try. I can never measure up.

I'm useless.

I have to do better.

I don't want to lose my daughter.

Eleven

Lita

I've got my down jacket on under my life jacket. My travel cup is filled with coffee and a generous amount of cinnamon-flavored creamer. I thought about putting in Bailey's instead, but I have to pace myself given it looks like there's going to be plenty of drinking going on all day today.

I took three Gravol tablets before we left home, and have the rest of the package in my pocket in case the first three wear off. I'm on one of the padded benches on the lower deck, trying to ignore the bobbing of the boat while I watch Nullah showing Finn how to bait the hook and pull out the right amount of line to set the Deep Six where the Fish Finder shows that the fish are. Apparently, they're deep, 200 feet, and at that depth in this area you need a Glow Chartreuse Snot Rocket Hoochie and a fluorocarbon leader and of course you want a Green Onion flasher with that. Well, naturally! I've heard all kinds of stuff like this before of course, but I think Finn is as impressed as I was the first time.

The boat itself is pretty impressive, a 37-foot Bayliner, flying bridge, queen size bed in the master stateroom (with its own head) fore, and a guest cabin aft. There's a very nice galley and a decent dining area, neither of which we'll be using today. Before setting out, we decided against eating on the boat and that even if we caught a fish, we'd save it for the gathering at home later. We're going to have an early lunch at the Dinghy Dock. This means we didn't have to get a bunch of groceries organized to take with us, and lunch at the Dinghy Dock always gets my vote.

Nullah says he thinks he has the speed right: slow enough to troll, fast enough that we don't catch dogfish. The lines are out and the rods are in their holders. Now it's sit back and wait for something to happen, and hope that if we do get a hit, a seal or sea lion doesn't steal it off the hook before we can land it.

The fishing report on the radio this morning claimed the Winchelsea Islands were hot, so that's where we are, chugging around in a holding pattern with half a dozen other boats. The aforementioned animals can be seen up on the rocks, lazily flapping their flippers. The trolling motor is quiet enough that we can hear them barking. Occasionally one lurches across the rocks and slips into the water. Nullah claims they're watching us as carefully as we're watching them, because they've learned a boat equals fishermen equals a chance for an easy meal. Nullah calls them lazy bastards. I call them resourceful and clever. But I do hope that if we get a fish on the line, they stay where they are. If they steal it, we'll have to keep fishing, and the less time we have to spend on the water, the better, in my opinion, even if it means getting to the Dinghy Dock early.

"How're you doin', babe?" Nullah asks.

"Fine," I tell him, and take a sip of coffee.

"She's prone to seasickness," Nullah tells Finn. "I think she'll get over it if we spend enough time on the boat."

"Not working so far," I mutter. I know Nullah loves boating, and that last comment of mine was maybe a little snarky. "But I'll keep trying," I add.

"'At's my girl," Nullah says as he gives my shoulder a rub and kisses the top of my head.

"How was your dinner last night?" I ask Finn after he refills his mug and slides onto the bench next to me.

"Man, the food was awesome. But I can't say the same for the company."

Nullah has taken the captain's chair at the helm, and swivels to look back at us. "No?"

"The wife was sweet, but that guy! Him and me did *not* hit it off. What a pompous ass! Unbelievable how he patted himself on the back and ran down the other lawyers, even those in his own firm. Talk about pushy! I practically had to hip check him out of the way before he'd let me out the door. I didn't actually *leave*. More like I *escaped*."

"Doesn't sound like a team player," Nullah opines.

"On paper he ticks all the boxes. He's definitely well qualified, but I doubt he plays well with others," Finn agrees. "I was wishing his wife would join the conversation more but she barely spoke more two sentences. What a meal she prepared! Cherries Jubilee for dessert, if you can believe it. Delicious!" He takes a sip of coffee then says, "You know how you ignite the liqueur when it's served?"

I nod. "In university I had a roommate who loved to make those flaming desserts. Cherries Jubilee, Crepes Suzette, Baked Alaska, you name it. Mostly just when we had guests of the male persuasion. Her mother drummed it into her that the way into a man's heart is through his stomach."

"What? Mothers teach their daughters to cook for their man?" Nullah interjects.

"My mother told me to just be myself. Turns out my talents lie in a different direction," I glare at him.

"And I'm glad about it."

"You are now. Wait till we're seventy."

"I'll be worn out long before that."

"No one feels sorry for you, mate," Finn chides, and chuckles. Then he turns to me and asks, "Do you like Cherries Jubilee?"

"Yeah. You?"

"First time I ever had it. I loved it! But when she lit mine, her blouse caught fire."

"Oh god, no! Was she hurt?"

"No, just a bit of the sleeve burned. I wrapped my napkin around her arm to smother it. Her husband just sat there. From the look on his face you would've thought she did it on purpose. And I had a sense that if I wasn't there, he would've left her to deal with it herself."

"My god, Finn," I exclaim, "good thing you knew what to do!"

"That's me, Super Finn to the rescue! Hey, he knows you, Lita."

"Oh, probably. It's a small town in some ways and not all that many lawyers, you know. What's his name?"

"He's with Jackson and Co. Derek Wilton."

I gasp.

He says, "I guess you know him."

"Yes. Very well."

"And another guess? You don't like him."

So many things I could say about Derek, none good, and none that relate to his suitability for what Nullah and Finn need. Finally I say, "I really haven't heard much about his work, but his character? I wouldn't recommend him even if he was the last lawyer in the world." Unprofessional of me, I know. But then, we're all friends here.

"He's a guy she used to date," Nullah explains, "back in college. And Carly was her roommate."

"Ahh! The roommate who made the flaming desserts."

"I thought Nullah said your Toronto lawyers had short-listed some lawyers for you. If they put Derek's name forward, they must've heard good things about him."

"They recommended the firm. I had a meeting with their senior partners and a few of the juniors. When I was leaving, Derek followed me to the door and invited me to dinner. He looks good as suits go and was well-spoken during our meeting, and walking me out? A dinner invite? I thought wow, he's a go-getter, maybe someone like that is a good guy to have working for you. But all the bragging! It's too bad I had dinner with him. Would've liked him more if I hadn't." Finn clicks his tongue, shrugs and says, "He's hard to like, but he's one of the best qualified guys on the list. We wouldn't spend much time with him. I think we should go ahead and have him vetted."

"Sure thing," Nullah agrees.

Just then the line on the rod nearest Finn goes zinging out and both men jump to their feet. Nullah cuts the engine, pulls the rod out of the holder and hands it to Finn. "Okay. Keep the tip up so the line stays tight!"

Twelve

Carly

My nose and the cut on my cheek stopped bleeding last night but my nose is really swollen and painful and I can't breathe through it. Besides that, I'm afraid the cut is going to leave a scar, so I want to go the clinic. Derek insists on taking me and even coming into the examining room with me. He's waiting in a chair at the foot of the table while the doctor is checking me out.

"Yes, you're right, this laceration is going to need closing," she says. "And you have a nasal fracture too. How did this happen?"

Derek says, "I was opening the bathroom door as she was coming out. She walked right into it! Poor girl! I need to be more careful." He reaches for my hand and looks at me with such a concerned expression anyone would think he meant it. "I'm sorry, honey! My fault, completely my fault!" His voice catches in a sob.

The doctor studies him for a moment, then asks, "This is going to take a while. Have you got anything else you need to do this morning, Mr. Wilton?"

"No. I just want to be here for her."

"I'll need to put her in another operatory. I'll ask you to go and wait in the waiting room, then."

"I'd really like to stay with her."

"I know, but there isn't room for her, my assistant and me, and you. Don't worry. She's in good hands."

"Okay then," Derek agrees. He squeezes my hand and leans in front of Doctor Evans to kiss my temple. "I'll be waiting right outside, sweetheart," he says, and leaves.

"I'll see you when we're set up in the operatory," Doctor Evans tells me, and follows him out.

In a few minutes, one of the receptionists comes to take me to a different room. I follow her through a maze of hallways to a larger room that has the examination table in the middle. "You can just hop up here," she tells me as she pats the paper sheet on the padded table. "Doctor Evans will be with you in a few minutes."

I look around, wondering how Doctor Evans thought there wouldn't be enough room for Derek to come in here with us. A nurse comes in with a tray, sets it on a stand on the far side of the table and says, "Hello. Had a bit of trouble, did you?"

A bit of trouble? You could say that. "Umm, yeah."

She raises the end section of the table and says, "Put your feet up and lean back here. Doctor Evans will just be a minute."

I do as she directs. She busies herself getting something out of the cabinets behind me, and then Doctor Evans comes in.

"Okay, Carly," Doctor Evans says, "I'm going to put a little freezing in your nose. It's out of alignment and we don't want you left with a crooked nose, so I'm going to straighten it, and it will need a splint as well as some packing. It's not a pleasant procedure, but once you're frozen at least it won't hurt. The spray, please Ashley?"

The nurse hands her the spray and Doctor Evans says, "This will feel a little funny." She sprays the medication into both nostrils, then hands the syringe back to the nurse. "Now then, this lac. I think it'll be best to close it with glue. We'll let your nose freeze while I do that." She works on cleaning the cut, then gluing it and gently pressing the edges together for the short time the glue takes to set.

"Now, no scratching or rubbing at this, and don't put a plaster over it. It should peel off in five or six days. Long before those black eyes have faded. There will be a scar, but it should be minor and will likely fade completely away in a few months."

Then she sets to work on my nose, asking Ashley for something called a nasal speculum, and filling my nostrils with packing. "That has to stay in place for a few days," she tells me. "You'll be a mouth breather for a while, I'm afraid." She grins and gives my shoulder a reassuring rub. She's placing the large adhesive patch over the bridge of my nose when two women come into the room.

The older of the two women holds up a badge and says, "Hi, Carly. I'm Detective Brennan. You can call me Doreen. And this is my partner, Detective Angela Weston."

"Oh..."

"We're here at the request of Doctor Evans. Your medical records show you've had a number of injuries in the past few years. She's concerned, so she asked us to come and talk to you."

Doctor Evans steps away and tells me, "You can sit up now."

I sit up, swallowing hard as my stomach clenches. I don't know what to say. If I tell them Derek did this to me, what will they do? Arrest him? It would only make it worse when he got out.

"Have you talked to my husband?" I ask.

"Not yet."

"Please don't. I'm fine. He had nothing to do with this. I'm just accident prone."

Detective Brennan is staring at me so intensely I have to look away. Finally, she says, "If your husband is hurting you, he won't stop, Carly. He'll promise to stop, all right, they always do. He'll tell you that he loves you like no one else ever could, that he'll never hurt you again. That he just lost control. But it's not about him losing control, it's about him *being in* control. Controlling *you*. There will always be a next time. There are hundreds of women killed by their significant others every year, in Canada alone. It's not an exaggeration to say any woman in an abusive relationship is at risk. We can take you to the women's shelter right now, today, if you want us to. There's support there—"

"But my daughter!"

"She's at home, is she?"

I nod. "Yes. But it's okay. We hardly ever leave her alone and she's very capable...she's ten. She's okay to stay home alone for a bit."

"Yes, of course. But we can go and get her."

I take several deep breaths, wondering what to do. Remembering Derek's threats that I would never be able to see Jennifer again if he kicked me out. What if I kicked him out? Would he go? Could I lock him out of the house? Would he wait until Jennifer left to go to school, pick her up on her way to the bus stop and take her to his mother in Phoenix? Maybe not right away, but sometime? She already has a passport. He could be across the border with her before I even realized she wasn't in school. Before they could even issue an Amber Alert. She's always liked going there. She might be happy to stay! I can't risk it. I shake my head slowly. "No."

"There is legal help available to you. And they can get him into anger management counselling so he—"

"He's not hurting me," I say. "He didn't do this. I walked into the bedroom door."

Detective Brennan stands quietly, just studying me, and after a moment says, "All right, then. Here's my card. You can call me any time. I mean any time, Carly." The detectives exchange knowing looks with Doctor Evans, and leave.

Doctor Evans looks at me, then pulls off her gloves, drops them in the trash, and comes back to face me again. She puts a hand on my forearm and says, "Your husband said it was the bathroom door you walked into, Carly."

"I meant bathroom. The door from our bedroom into the bathroom."

"They can help you, you know. I can help you, Carly."

I shake my head and fight off tears.

"Okay," she says, and sighs. "The packing will need to come out in a few days, as I said. You can come to the drop-in clinic or make an appointment." She's biting her lip as she pats my arm, then turns and leaves the room.

I compose myself before I slide down off the table, nod to Ashley, and leave.

Through the waiting room windows I see Derek pacing back and forth on the sidewalk outside. When as soon as I'm outside, he hurries to me and engulfs me in a hug. I have no urge to hug him back and let my arms hang at my sides.

He releases me and takes my hand to lead me to the car. "Don't you look a sight with those black eyes and that big fuckin' patch on your nose!" He goes to the passenger door and opens it for me. "You won't be going anywhere for a while."

"I have to shop," I tell him as I get in my seat and buckle in.

"Nope! I'll do the shopping." He closes my door, goes around to the driver's side and gets behind the wheel. He buckles up, then starts the engine, but before shifting into gear, he reaches for my hand and gives it a squeeze. "I'm so sorry, honey. You know I love you! I would never have hurt you if I hadn't had so much to drink. I saw how he was looking at you, and I lost control! I know you're attractive to other men, and I know you can't help but look back. It's only natural."

"I wasn't looking back," I mumble, although I know it's a lie.

He doesn't acknowledge that I said anything, just backs the car out of the parking space and drives to the exit. As he watches for traffic to clear, he says, "And then there was him taking off like that, wouldn't even name a date that I might expect to hear something. You know what? I bet Lita badmouthed me."

I remember Finn asked Derek if he knew Lita. If he had been talking to Lita about Derek, he wouldn't have had to ask.

"I don't think so—"

"Well, I wouldn't put it past her. You shouldn't have cut her off like you did."

"But you said—"

"I think you should call her up. Apologize and mend the fences. Get her out for dinner again sometime. Or maybe a few drinks some afternoon. Get her to bring her boyfriend. He's the partner, right? She can put the two of us together. Wouldn't hurt my chances at all. In fact it would be a real foot in the door!"

I'm gobsmacked. Now he wants me to mend fences with Lita? After how adamant he was that I stop seeing her?

"But I thought she... If I invite her again, won't she think you... I mean, won't that encourage her?"

"Sure, but if her boyfriend's there, she won't dare make a pass at me." He turns to face me for a second, his face alight with the happiest smile I've seen in months. "Call her up and arrange something. But of course, not until that mess on your face is cleared up." He focuses his attention to the traffic, turns up the volume on the stereo and whistles along.

Lita back in our lives? I'm hurt, sad, and angry at her years of deception, but I have missed her. Maybe I'll get a chance to talk to her alone. Ask her why she has been trying to get Derek away from me. And then it hits me: maybe it would be a good thing if she succeeded. Maybe she would dump her boyfriend and Derek would move in with her.

But Derek's right, probably she hasn't been solo all those times she came to our place alone. Finn said he met her the last time he was here, but he didn't say how long ago that was. If it was more than a couple of months, she would've had this boyfriend the last time she came for dinner. Why didn't she say anything? It must not be serious. But then, serious enough to meet his business partner? Still. She's been after Derek for years, and she changes men as often as her underwear. Maybe because she's still hung up on Derek? This boyfriend won't be a problem.

After a double date, then maybe I make a date with her for lunch, just the two of us, and have Derek show up in my place.

I put my sunglasses on, careful of my nose, as my mind whirls with ideas.

Thirteen

Lita

My phone rings and I glance at the screen. That unknown number again. The caller is persistent. You'd think at some point they would leave a voicemail. I conclude they don't because the caller needs to talk to me directly in order to sell me something. I touch the button on the side of the phone to stop the ringing and decide that the next time it happens, I'll block the number.

Even if the call wasn't from an unknown number, I wouldn't answer it because I'm in the middle of digesting a detailed adjuster's report. I always enjoy the reports from this particular adjuster because they're so organized, readable, and smart. This file involves a run-of-the-mill slip and fall claim. The plaintiff claims to be so badly injured she's unable to work. Store surveillance video shows the woman falling and a staffer coming to her aid. A squashed grape is located on the floor, three yards from the bunk where grapes are displayed. It couldn't have gotten that far just rolling off the bunk, so another shopper must have dropped it. The sweep logs show the area was swept four minutes earlier, well within the time the courts have found fulfills the store's duty of care, but the video of the sweep shows the young staffer hurrying through the produce section, changing direction often and dodging customers. He swept around someone selecting onions in the area where the plaintiff fell. Understandable of course, but it means plaintiff's counsel could argue the grape was not dropped after the sweep, but was missed in that sweep. We'll argue the duty of care was met, but a judge may not agree, so we'll be left challenging the severity of the woman's injury. I'm reading what the adjuster has to say about the woman's activities, flipping back and forth to the medical records, when the phone rings again.

I glance at my phone and see it's that unknown caller again. They usually only call once a day. This is getting damned annoying. I push the button to stop the ringing and get back to my report, when the chime for voicemail sounds. Well, what do you know? My curiosity is piqued. I decide I need a coffee break, so I go to the break room and make myself a cup before coming back to my desk to listen to the message.

"Hi Lita. It's Carly."

I'M PERCHED ON A STOOL at the island, drinking wine and watching Nullah squeeze a lemon over the salmon filets he poached. I love the way Nullah prepares salmon, with a sprinkling of fresh dill and plenty of hollandaise sauce. I have to admit my diet has improved considerably since he's been in my life. I think I may have to buy bigger clothes.

My contribution to dinner was making the Super Greens salad from a bag and boiling water for Uncle Ben's Fast and Fancy Fine Herb and Wild Rice pilaf. For his part, Nullah is impressed with my uncanny ability to source gourmet accompaniments now that I've made him aware it's a life skill that took years of trial and error to acquire.

"Carly called me today," I tell him. "She has a new number. I guess that's why she never responded to any of my texts."

"I didn't know you were still trying to connect with her. Just since Finn said he met her?"

"No, I gave up before that."

"You'd think she would've given you her new number, though."

"You'd think so."

"So, what did she have to say?"

"I didn't call her back yet. Her message was that she'd like to get together. She talked about 'we' as in 'we should get together', so I'm guessing that means Derek's included. I bet he's the push behind it."

"Could be."

"Could be? Absolutely is! Finn mentioned me to him, so now the conniving bastard wants to make nice. It's not me he's interested in, it's you. He probably wants to suck up to you in hopes you'll put in a good word for him with Finn."

"That's what I love about you, babe, you always think the best of everyone."

"Come on, Nullah," I say with a click of my tongue, "what other possible reason could there be for Carly wanting to connect now? She's had months to get back in touch and there's been nothing but crickets. They find out my boyfriend is a partner in a company looking for a lawyer—and that there's a pretty decent retainer involved—and all of a sudden she wants to get together? Coincidence? I don't think so."

"I know, cops and lawyers don't believe in coincidence. You're probably right."

"I am right."

"So call her back and find out what it's about."

"I'm not going to just up and ask her if she's calling because Derek put her up to it."

"Maybe she just wants to talk to you. From what you've told me, she doesn't have a lot of friends. Maybe you were her only friend."

"Pretty hard to foster friendships when you're married to that controlling bastard! He never lets us have two minutes alone." I sip my wine while Nullah takes the frying pan off the stove and puts a filet on the plate in front of me. When he's served himself and set the pan back on the stove, he comes around to sit next to me.

"Well, if you want my opinion, I think you should call and see what she wants. She knows you and I are together, so she might suggest we come for dinner. You said he has a boat, right? You can say we'd prefer to meet them for lunch at the Dinghy Dock. That way we aren't trapped with them. And I think it's about time you had a lesson on driving the boat, besides. A nice easy trip to the Dinghy Dock for your first time at the helm is a good start."

"You want me to take it out of the boat shed? Drive it all the way over there and dock it?"

"I'll show you how to start it, but I'll take it out, and once we're clear of the marina, you can take over. Docking at the Dinghy Dock is not 'all the way'; it's ten minutes maybe, and about as easy as it could be. You can do it."

"I don't see why you're so anxious for me to learn how to drive it. I'll never take it out without you."

"It's just a good skill to have, like driving a stick shift. What if something happens to the driver and you have to take over to get back to safety? What if I was incapacitated somehow? Or fell overboard? You have to know how to get back to me. Back to safety."

"There's a radio."

"Sure, and I'll give you a lesson on how to use that, too, but would you be able to tell them where we were?"

"Doesn't the chart plotter show where you are?"

"Uh huh. But by the time help came, I'd drown."

"You always wear that floater jacket."

"Suppose for some reason I didn't have it on."

"You're a good swimmer. You can tread water."

"In sixty-degree water, I'd die of hypothermia."

"Why would you fall overboard in the first place?"

"Supposing I was taking a leak and a rogue wave jostled the boat. You know half the guys that drown while they're out fishing are found with their flies undone."

"If you pee overboard when there's two heads on the boat and you aren't wearing your floater jacket, you deserve to drown."

"My god, woman!"

"I know. You think I'm stubborn." I stand and go to the fridge to refill my wine glass.

"I've never said you were stubborn."

"Okay, determined, then." I set my wine at my plate and ask, "You want another glass? Or a beer?"

"No thanks. I need a clear head to argue with you."

Fourteen

Carly

We've agreed to meet Lita and her boyfriend at the Dinghy Dock for lunch today. It's December, so they said the place won't be too busy, even though much of the deck is closed for the season, there is a heated area so we can sit inside or out, our choice.

Rather than making the trip in the boat, we drove to downtown Nanaimo, parked in the parkade, walked to the Boat Basin, and now we're waiting to board the shuttle boat for the ten-minute crossing to the Dinghy Dock.

"I don't see why they were so adamant about going to the fucking Dinghy Dock," Derek mutters. "Eighteen bucks for the two of us to take the ferry, probably another twenty for the sitter, on top of the cost of a meal? The food better be good."

"We could've taken the boat."

"Go through Dodd Narrows in this weather and in an ebb tide? Jesus, Carly, it's a wonder you can dress yourself. Anyway. Meeting this Smith guy will be worth it. What's his name? Nelly?"

"Nullah."

"What kind of name is that?"

I shrug. I hope he doesn't ask Lita's boyfriend that question, or slip up and call him Nelly. Although with a name like that, he's probably used to people wondering about it. "Can't you put this all on your expense account?" I ask.

"Yeah. But that's not the point. This is damned inconvenient when we could just as easily have gone to the Lighthouse Bistro. Or better yet, the Crow and Gate. We don't need to see the water. It's not like we're tourists."

"Maybe they like an excuse to get out on the boat."

"Well, they can do it some other time when it doesn't inconvenience us."

The passenger ferry chugs into its slot next to the dock. A few people get off, and we're among the half dozen or so who get in. We take seats along the side. The little boat leaves the dock for the ten-minute crossing at the posted departure time.

When we approach the pub, we see a couple of small runabouts moored to the wharf, and one boat big enough to be called a yacht.

"Jeez," Derek says quietly, "look at that cabin cruiser! I get this retainer and a couple more good clients, and that'll be my next boat."

"I guess they're not here yet," I say. "We're not late, but knowing Lita, they will be. Otherwise they would have been on this ferry."

When the ferry pulls into its assigned mooring just a couple of yards from the pub's entrance, we climb off. About half of our fellow passengers head around behind the pub and up the stairs to destinations on Protection Island proper. We follow the other passengers into the pub. To my surprise, I spot Lita at a table on the far side. She looks up, smiles, and waves. I lift my hand in acknowledgement.

With her is a big man, his wavy black hair shoulder-length. He's so much bigger than she is that he dwarfs her. He's movie-star handsome in a Jason Momoa kind of way, which is not surprising since Lita always attracted the good-looking ones, but what is surprising is how dark his skin is. My insides contract and I draw a quick breath. With all the derogatory things I've heard Derek say about non-whites, I have a feeling this lunch won't go well. The unusual name may only be the start.

"There they are," I tell Derek, and lead the way through the tables.

The man gets to his feet on our approach, and gives a slight bow. "Hi," he says. "I'm Nullah. You must be Carly."

"Yes. Pleased to meet you, Nullah."

"Pleased to meet you." He turns to Derek and says, "Derek?" He doesn't reach for a handshake, and Derek will likely hold that against him even though it's fallen out of favor since the pandemic.

But Derek doesn't reach his hand out, either. His face is set in a frown. "Derek," he confirms.

"Have a seat," Lita says.

I take the chair across from Lita, which leaves Derek sitting across from Nullah. I ask, "Have you been waiting long?"

"Nope. We just got here a few minutes ago so we haven't even got a drink yet."

Nullah waves the server over and I ask for a glass of house white. Derek overrides me, makes a show of studying the menu to see what wines are on offer while the captive server waits, asks Lita what she prefers, and ends up ordering a forty-dollar bottle of chardonnay for the two of us. Then he asks the server what's on tap. As usual, he hums and haws, then has to hear what bottled beer they have, and when she's rattled off the list, finally settles on a local craft brew.

We study the menus while we're waiting for drinks, and Derek asks, "So you got here just before we did. You didn't come on the passenger ferry, then."

"No. We came on Nullah's boat," Lita tells him.

"Which one is it?"

"That one there," Nullah says, and points to the cabin cruiser moored right outside our window.

I can almost hear Derek choke. When he recovers, he says, "That's a lot like my boat. What's that, a Bayliner? Thirty footer?"

"Thirty-seven," Nullah says.

"Oh. Thirty-seven. You had it long?"

"About a year. I looked for quite a while to find this one. Didn't want to buy a new one and get killed with depreciation. Was lucky enough to get it from a guy right here in Nanaimo. In good shape, too. He'd just done a bunch of work on it, flooring, and so on. If you're interested, I'll show it to you after lunch."

"Nullah, we don't have that much time, remember? Maybe we order our food, and you can give him a tour while we're waiting for it to come."

"Oh yeah. Good idea," Nullah agrees. "You do a lot of boating, Derek?"

"Not as much as I'd like to. Our daughter's discovered boys so she doesn't want to go out with me. I'd like to spend a few weeks and tour Haida Gwaii and some of the inlets up north. I guess that'll have to wait until she changes her mind. Or brings a boyfriend with her. What about you?"

"I mostly just fished with my old boat. It wasn't one you'd like to take very far. And I haven't had this one long enough to do more than day trips. But we're planning on spending a couple of weeks heading up to Bute Inlet next summer," Nullah says.

"Bute Inlet? That's something I've wanted to do for a while. I'll go with you," Derek suggests.

"Oh, sure, but I've got a couple of mates coming with me so the bunks are all taken."

"I meant, I'll take my boat. Carly doesn't like being on the boat so she can stay home with Jennifer."

"Sure," Nullah agrees, "the more the merrier."

"Well, wives are going along," Lita says. "You can't be the only guy who doesn't bring his family, Derek. Carly and Jennifer would just have to come too. A ten-year-old doesn't call the shots, surely."

Good old outspoken Lita! It sure didn't take long for her to get snotty with Derek.

"Of course not. It's just that Carly doesn't like going out in the boat. Do you, Carly?" He gives my foot a stomp.

"It's, um, no, I don't," I agree.

The server appears at the table with our drinks and we all order lunch. When Nullah and Derek go out to look at Nullah's boat, I make a point of avoiding eye contact with Lita. I want to ask her why she made a pass at Derek, but I'm at a loss to know how to bring it up. Finally she reaches across the table and covers my hand with hers.

"Carly," she says, "you have a scar on your cheek! What happened?"

I pull my hand out from under hers and touch my cheek, wondering how she noticed. It's still a little angry-looking but I thought the makeup covered it. "I, er, walked into a door."

"Really? How'd that happen?"

"Oh, you know, woke up in the middle of the night to go pee and didn't turn any lights on." I pick up the dessert menu. "Death By Chocolate sounds good," I say, hoping to change the subject.

She's quiet for a minute. I don't look at her, but I feel her eyes on me.

"Why did it take you so long to contact me?" she asks at last. "Why did you ignore all my texts? I thought you were mad at me after dinner that time, but I have no idea why."

I study her face for a second and read nothing there but sincerity. "You have no idea? Derek told me what you did," I say.

"What I did?"

"What you did."

"What did he say I did?"

I take a deep breath, breathe out, and say, "You tried to kiss him."

"*What?*"

"You tried to kiss him. When he wanted to show you his boat. On the trail. On the steps down to the boat. You grabbed him and tried to kiss him. You've never given up on him, not ever, in all the years since he dumped you and married me you've been after him." I'm speaking so fast I hardly have time to take a breath. She just sits there shaking her head until I finally run out of words.

"That's not what happened, Carly."

"Yes it is! I saw you when he put his hand on your leg. You moved your leg so his hand would slide up under your skirt."

"Carly, think about it. How could I do that? It's bloody near impossible. He tried to put his hand up my skirt. And down on the trail, *he* grabbed *me*. I can barely tolerate being near him, so I sure as *fuck* wouldn't make a pass at him. If I wanted him I wouldn't have dumped him years ago."

"He said he broke up with you."

"So why did he keep calling me? He was practically stalking me, remember? It was on one of those unannounced visits that he somehow convinced you to go out with him."

"He seemed so lost. When he broke up with you, he was alone here. No family even."

"As if he ever gave a shit about his family! What a manipulator!"

"He said he was falling in love with me."

"I'm not saying that's impossible, Carly, you are very loveable. But he's a pig! I warned you about him."

"I thought it was just because, well, like he said, you were put out because he dumped you."

"*Pffft!* He dumped me? What an ass. I couldn't believe it when he got you pregnant right away so you'd marry him. You seemed happy, so I didn't say anything but I think it was deliberate. What did he say? *'I've been around enough to know what to do, it doesn't feel good to wear a condom'*, correct?"

My head spins. How could she possibly know about that? "How did you—"

"He tried to talk me out of taking the pill. Concern for my health because there might be a link to breast cancer or some other ridiculous reason. Concern for my health, my ass. I think he might even have stolen my pills when I refused. I know they were gone. Remember I asked you if you knew where they were?"

"Um, no."

"It was right after that, that I dumped him. Remember?"

"I guess I do remember that."

"Anyway, I would never have come to your place for dinner if it wasn't for the fact it was the only way I could see you, since you never want to meet for lunch or anything. You, not Derek! Although he never gives us a minute alone. It's astonishing he's left the two of us here now!"

"But..." I glance out the window and see Derek and Nullah on the back deck of the boat. Derek is looking directly at us, his face creased in a frown. Lita follows my gaze and takes her hand off mine.

She says, "You look so serious. Smile, honey. Pretend we're sharing a joke!" She starts with a fake little laugh and goes cross-eyed as she looks at me. In a heartbeat we're both genuinely laughing.

When we see the men climb out of the boat and start toward the door, Lita says, "We need to talk some more, Carly. From now on, answer my texts."

"I can't really text on my new phone," I tell her. "And Derek wouldn't like it."

"So don't tell him," she advises. "But you wanted to meet with us now. Is it because of Nullah's company?"

I fiddle with my napkin-wrapped cutlery, and quietly admit it. "Yes."

"And what do you mean, Derek wouldn't like you calling me? He doesn't want you calling me?"

"No."

She blows out a long breath and says, "But he doesn't have to know about it. Call when you can."

"What if he checks my phone to see who I've called?"

"Use your landline."

"We don't have a landline anymore."

"Oh? Well, then, delete your recents."

"I don't know how."

"If you can't figure it out, then tell him you're checking to see if there's any news from Nullah. And there's always email."

"I don't... I can't email. I don't have a computer. And all my phone does is, er, phone."

"Call when you can, then."

The men come through the door. I give Lita a quick nod of agreement just as they rejoin our table. As Derek sits and pulls his chair up to the table, he looks at me and says, "You gals sure had your heads together. What were you talking about? Looked like it must have been funny."

"Girl talk," I tell him.

Derek frowns and says, "Since when is menstrual cramps funny?"

"You think that's all women have to talk about?" Lita asks. "I was telling her Nullah had never heard me fart. He still wouldn't have, except one night when we were getting out of the hot tub, I bent over to get my croc out from under the step and with no warning, just ripped one."

I'm taken aback but force a smile. Derek frowns.

Nullah chuckles and says, "I was facing her way, too. It was an impressive treble fart, and the smell was enough to gag a maggot."

"Don't lie," Lita says, "my farts smell delicious. Like chili."

"Maybe the chili you make," he says.

I draw a quick breath. I would have been hurt and insulted by a comment like that, but Lita shrugs, obviously not offended.

Derek forces an awkward chuckle. I know I'm going to hear more about this later. I'm sure he'll have an opinion about me laughing at something so vulgar.

Lita says, "Hey, have you guys started surfing the net with your TV? I didn't know you could do that. Nullah has ours all set up. Very nice, especially for YouTube."

I feel a jolt of interest. I could use the TV to get on the internet? "Can we do that, Derek?"

"No. We don't have a Smart TV.

"You don't?" Lita asks. "I thought you had the latest and best of everything."

I don't miss the sarcasm. From the look Nullah gives her, he doesn't either. "You don't need to ditch a perfectly good tv to upgrade. There's a gadget that makes any TV smart," he says. "Just get a TV box. Costs about fifty bucks."

"If I thought I needed a smart TV, I'd buy one. I wouldn't piss around with a box," Derek says.

The server brings our food and we're quiet as we all dig in to our meals. I slice open my fish so it can cool. It's soggy and doughy, but I don't say anything. My mind is abuzz. I could surf the net on the TV? And what about Lita's shocking allegation about Derek's lies? I think she might be right. Derek kept coming around for weeks after they weren't seeing each other. If he was falling in love with me, like he said, why did he always ask for Lita?

I no longer think it will be possible to get the two of them together. Not just because she seems to be telling the truth about how she feels about Derek, but, well, Nullah. He's obviously successful, looks at her as if she's the sun and the moon, and she's looking back the same way. Who could blame her?

From the looks he's been giving Nullah and the lie about his boat, I'd say Derek finds him threatening. Between mouthfuls, he's telling Nullah about all the exams he took to get admitted to the bar in Canada, how difficult they were and how he doubts any of his colleagues could have passed them.

"We know you're very well qualified," Nullah tells him. "We're looking seriously at your CV."

"Taking long enough," Derek says.

"I know, waiting's hard. We want to be sure it's a good fit because we want to foster a long-term relationship."

"Sure," Derek grumbles, and attacks his steak sandwich.

He so anxious to impress Nullah that there's an edge of desperation in his voice even I can't miss.

Lita is watching me with a perplexed expression. She says, "So, Carly, let's get together for lunch sometime next week, okay? Just us girls. So we can catch up."

I nod.

"I'm going to hold you to that," she insists.

"WHERE ON EARTH DID she dig up that asshole?" Derek wonders. We've just left the pub. While we watch the passenger ferry approach, Nullah and Lita on their big boat slip away from the wharf and Lita waves. Derek smiles and waves back, then says, "He looks like a fuckin' illegal alien. Is he Mexican? How'd he wind up here, and where'd he get the money for a boat like that? Notice how he bragged about it being a thirty-seven footer? And he owns fitness clubs? Wonder if he's a drug dealer."

"How could he be a drug dealer?"

"How else could a wetback own all that?"

"Did he tell you he's Mexican?"

"Didn't have to. I grew up in Arizona, remember? I've seen enough greasers in my life to know one when I see one."

"He doesn't have that kind of an accent, though. I think he sounds more like an Aussie."

"Maybe he's part of a cartel," Derek continues as if I haven't spoken. "It would explain why he has that boat. Just cruise down the coast outside the US and Canadian territorial waters, fill the hold with Mexican Brown, and cruise on back to Nanaimo. How else could he get that kind of money?"

"He said he got the North American distributorship for that line of workout equipment when the company was just starting out."

"Yeah, well, he would say something like that. Make up a cover story. Bet he deals drugs out of those clubs. I think I'll report him."

"You mean call the cops and tell them you think he's dealing drugs, with no proof?"

Derek snorts loudly, shakes his head and frowns at me. "Why do you think the cops have that anonymous tip line, dummy? They're always looking for tips. They'd send an undercover guy in to make a buy and they'd have the proof. Easy peasy. In fact, the more I think about it, it would carry more weight if they knew it was me, one of the top lawyers in town, tipping them off. There may even be a reward."

"A reward?"

"Yeah, a reward."

"But what if you're right and the cops, er, bust him? If he gets arrested, how will that help you get the retainer for the business?"

"You don't think Mr. Finnegan is involved in it, do you? He's got more class than that. I bet he doesn't even know he's hooked up with drug runners. With Nelly out of the way, maybe I just slide in and take his place."

"You mean, run the fitness clubs? But they'd have others in the company that already know the business—"

"After what they'd owe me for getting rid of him for them? Pfft! What do you know? Nothing."

I draw a quick breath and turn away.

The ferry chugs into its slip, and when the incoming passengers have offloaded, we're among the few who get on for the return trip to Nanaimo.

We're back in our car heading home, and I think Derek has forgotten about Lita's fart story until he says, "So, you laugh at Lita's vulgar story about farting? Something she should be embarrassed about? Instead she acts as if she's proud of it."

"No, she just thought it was funny—"

"Well, it's not funny. And you're going to meet her for lunch?"

I look straight ahead, wondering what his take on that will be. I know he doesn't want the two of us together, or me even calling her, so what is he thinking about a girls lunch? Will he want me to cancel? Or want to go with me?

"That's good," he says, nodding vigorously. "It's good. But keep to business."

"I will," I assure him.

"If you say anything—and I mean *anything*—that makes me look bad. Anything that tanks my chances with that big stupid fucker—"

"I won't!" I swallow hard. "Why would I say anything to make you look bad? I want you to get that assignment as much as you do!"

"It's not just an assignment," he scowls. "It's called a retainer."

"Retainer, then. I want you to get it. I'm sure you'll get it."

"You're sure? Well, that's just such a fuckin' comfort. I'll be sure and pass your opinion along to the boss."

We ride along in silence until we reach the Cedar Road turnoff, when he asks, "How could you laugh at that fart story? It's disgusting. And it's disgusting you laughed."

"I was, umm, the way she was laughing that was funny. You know laughter is infectious," I tell him. "I know it's a good connection for you. I had to go along with it. And you'll want me to keep, er, being friends with her?"

"Yeah," he nods. "Keep in touch. Having a friend like Nelly will be a really good connection."

"I'm going to need the car then, Derek. Maybe I should have my own now. Not a new one, just something inexpensive and reliable.

Maybe one of those they have out in front of the tire shop with the For Sale signs in the window. We could get one today. We'll be driving right past it anyway."

"Today? Don't be stupid. I won't have my wife driving around in one of those beaters, plus I can't afford it. It's not a purchase I would rush into, even if I thought you actually needed a vehicle. She can drive you."

"I can't ask her to come all the way out to our place to pick me up."

"You can walk over to the café and meet her there, then."

"Still, that's at least a twenty-minute drive from her office. She wouldn't have a long enough lunch break."

"Take a cab. You're a lousy driver anyway, and a cab makes more sense. No cash outlay to buy a car. No payments. No insurance. No gas or maintenance. Just call a cab when you need one. Way more cost effective than buying a car. I'll set up an account with the taxi company so you can just sign a chit. You don't even have to pay them." He hums for another few minutes before continuing, "You can take a cab when you shop for groceries, too." He grins and nods as he thinks it through. "That'll really free up my weekends. No more waiting for you at the store. I can take Jennifer where she wants to go. I'll join the golf club. I can go to the gym without wasting time at the grocery store and you can get your groceries whenever."

He'll join the golf club? That would cost as much as one of those used cars the tire shop has for sale. But instead of pointing that out, I say, "You don't need to go to the grocery store with me, Derek. You never did before. And I don't know why you don't let me shop in the evenings."

"Seriously? You're going to buy lettuce that's been out on the shelf all day?"

"I don't think—"

"That's right, you don't think. And you only shopped without me when Jennifer was with you, like when you took her to swimming. So you couldn't dilly dally around in the store for hours."

"I don't stay in the store for hours. I can shop by myself."

"Sure, and you buy all sorts of crap we don't need. I can't afford the grocery bills if you're left to buy whatever. We'll give it a try. If you bring home a bunch of useless crap—"

"What useless crap?"

"Don't interrupt!" He glares at me, and continues, "Five kinds of flour comes to mind. Not just groceries, either. Cookbooks and magazines. And knickknacks! We need more cat ornaments? More little potted plants?"

A song he likes comes on the radio and he turns up the volume. He hums along, then suddenly turns the volume down again and says, "I'm going to need a new boat. I can't go boating with Nelly and his friends in a cuddy cabin. What kind of impression would that make?"

"But that's months away. Next spring, or summer. If you get him arrested—"

"Those things take time. Maybe years, even, if they want to take down the whole ring. I'll be buddying up to him in the meantime. Might even get more inside info for the cops that way."

Now he's going to be an informant? "But if you're right and he's involved with drugs, that's dangerous!"

"I know how to handle myself." He squirms in his seat as if to sit taller, and I realize he's picturing himself as some kind of 007. And buying a big boat when just minutes ago, he said he couldn't afford a used car? "I'll get at least a forty-footer," he says with a nod. "Watch Nelly squirm when I tell him mine's bigger than his."

"But you said we owe too much on credit cards. And with our house payments and payments on this SUV, how can we afford another new boat?"

"It's not another boat, dummy, I'll trade in the one I already have. And remortgage the house."

"Remortgage our house? I thought we were thinking of selling it and buying something more affordable."

"When was that, five years ago? I can't live in a vinyl box in a subdivision, you know that! I need to live in a house as good as Jackson's. Well, maybe not Jackson's, but Duffy's for sure." He scowls and shakes his head. "I won't have to remortgage. I'll get a second mortgage. And I have a line of credit. And Jennifer can start going to public school."

"But Derek, you wanted Jennifer in that school because Mr. Jackson's kids go there. And you wouldn't really make Jen change schools, would you? Leave all her friends? And the band? You know how much she's looking forward to the trip to Ottawa for the band competition!"

"That would be a last resort."

"But—"

He holds up his hand and snarls, "Enough!"

I'll have to wait for another opportunity to bring up the subject of the tv box and surfing the net on the big screen. This is definitely not the time, not with all the crazy thoughts that must be stewing in his head. Besides, I'm sure he'd realize that I'd be able to go online too. He's already taken my iPhone away to stop that. I feel my shoulders droop as I realize it's a non-starter.

Then I let my mind roll back over everything Lita said. That Derek lies. Maybe it's Lita that's lying. But she knew about the condom thing. She knew exactly what Derek said about that. And she reminded me he kept coming around after they split. If he dumped her, would he do that? But he said he was falling in love with me.

He didn't have to come around. He could've phoned to ask me for a date.

It hits me with the force of a charging bull: Derek is a liar and he's been lying to me for a long time. Worse, he believes his own lies. And I've let him get away with it all these years.

He's right. I am a dummy.

Fifteen

Lita

"I told you, Derek is a jerk. He actually said the upholstery in the boat was due for an update?"

"That he did. Well, not in those words, exactly," Nullah says. "The way he put it was, his boat isn't second hand like mine, so the upholstery isn't so outdated. I guess he's so well-fixed he doesn't mind pissing away thousands of dollars on depreciation."

"Remember when your nose was out of joint because I didn't take you to dinner at their place? I warned you."

"My nose wasn't out of joint," he says. "I just thought it was weird."

"Toe-may-toe, toe-*maaw*-toe."

"Okay, maybe I was a little miffed," he allows, his dark brows drawing together in a frown. "Well, anyway, you were right. Finn was right. He's an asshole and not someone I want to spend any time with. I hope the P.I. we hired to check into the guy comes up with a reason to drop him from the list."

"Why isn't it enough that you and Finn both dislike him?"

He shrugs. "I guess because he ticks all the boxes. Finn's really cautious. Doesn't want another lawsuit alleging discriminatory hiring practices. And if I read him right, Derek's just the kind of asshole to sue."

"I don't think a white male could claim discrimination. You're allowed to hire who you want, so long as you don't say we hired someone younger or who isn't gay or something like that."

"You're probably right. I'll call Finn and let him know the PI can down tools because I met the guy and don't like him. I'm the one that lives here. I'm the one that would have to interact with him."

"Right."

"And that trip to Bute Inlet? We'll be leaving without telling him."

"I'm with you," I sigh. "But at least the food was good today. My salad was, anyway. How were your ribs?"

"As good as always."

"I don't think Carly enjoyed her fish, going by how she poked away at it. I doubt she enjoyed anything about the lunch, for that matter. She looked embarrassed when Derek was telling you how much better he is than the other lawyers in his firm. But lunch wasn't a complete bust. At least I found out why she'd been giving me the cold shoulder. That asshole told her I tried to kiss him."

"What?" His dark eyes flash. "Now I wish we *had* offered them a ride back to town so I could toss the prick overboard."

"That's the second time you've suggested throwing him overboard," I say. "Is that your solution for every problem?"

"You have to agree it's worth considering. One lunch and I've had more than enough of him. My god, he really thinks the sun shines out of his asshole, doesn't he? I was glad you came up with the excuse that we were meeting another friend over on Mudge Island so we didn't have to spend more time with them."

"Carly's okay. At least when he's not around."

"Yeah, she's okay. Too bad he dominated the entire conversation. It's obvious he was the push behind us getting together."

"I'm worried about her. You should've seen the look on her face when she saw Derek watching us from the boat. You know, it's the first time in years he's left the two of us alone. Almost like he never wants to give us a chance for girl talk. You know, intimacy. I don't know what that black look was about, but I have a sense that she's afraid of him."

"You think he gets physical?"

"Maybe. He slapped me once. She's browbeaten if nothing else. There's no other reason for her to react the way she did just because he was looking at us. And she said he wouldn't like her calling me. That's why I made such a point about the two of us getting together for lunch this week. He can't put a kibosh in it now, not without offending you. He always was a controlling bastard, and him lying about me trying to kiss him! Plus it's been years since she had her own car, so she's stuck out there day in, day out. It's as if she's under house arrest."

"She could call you when he's not around."

"I don't know if it works like that. I don't know if she would dare do something that he disapproved of. Would you believe he checks her phone to see who she's been calling?"

"Really? She needs to tell him to fuck the hell off."

"Yeah, she does, but she won't."

"Why would anyone put up with that?"

"I know, hey? It's hard to understand his hold over her. He always was the dominant one in their relationship but now it's like he's her jailer."

"I'm having a hard time imagining the two of you together."

"You mean me and Derek?"

"Well, that too, but I was thinking of you and Carly."

"She was the quiet one, that's true. I guess she usually just went along with whatever I wanted, but we had lots of fun together. We used to party like demons, and she always joined in what ever we were doing. She'd never sit there like a bump on a log like she did today. If she had enough to drink, she could even get pretty risqué."

"That would be a different Carly from the one I just met," Nullah agrees. "I suppose if he thinks you encourage her to stand up to him, he won't be happy about her connecting with you."

"That's probably it. But now he can't object to her meeting me for lunch this week. Not with you there to witness the fact she agreed to it. And maybe she'll be different when it's just the two of us."

"He'll coach her on what to say. Maybe get her to remind you that he's the smartest lawyer on Vancouver Island and possibly in the world. His arm must ache from patting himself on the back. *Argghh*! I see why Finn said he wouldn't buy a used car from the smarmy bastard."

"Jeez, from the look on your face I wouldn't have guessed you felt that way."

Nullah gives me such a shocked look I laugh, stand and kiss his ear. "I'm teasing. You were fine. I'm sure Carly liked you a lot. And I'm sure she realizes her husband doesn't measure up."

He loops an arm around me and gives me a squeeze and a quick kiss, but then releases me so he can have both hands on the helm. "You should sit back down," he says, and cuts the motor as we approach the channel marker at the entrance to the marina. "I wonder if you should get involved with those two. She has to grow some balls and stand up for herself."

"I think that's awfully difficult. Maybe having a friend on her side would help her do that."

"I wonder... She admitted he wanted this lunch because he thought it would help him, right?"

"Yeah."

"You don't think he'll blame her when we tell him he's not going to get it?"

"Oh! I hadn't thought of that. If he does...if he *is* an abuser...what if he hurts her?"

"Hmm."

"Maybe you could let him down easy."

"How to you sugar coat *we think you're a fuckin' asshole and we wouldn't want you if you were the last lawyer on earth*?"

"I don't know," I admit.

Nullah pulls past the entrance to his boat house, puts the engines in reverse, I put out the bumpers, and he neatly swings the boat around to back in. I take the aft mooring rope and jump out. Nullah follows, fixes the mooring ropes to the cleats, and closes the boat house doors.

As we're walking back up the wharf and through the gate to the parking lot, he says, "So. What if I just told him we'd re-assessed our needs and instead of offering a retainer, we were hiring someone in-house. Finn said Derek made a comment about you being an in-house lawyer for an insurance company. Like it's a good gig for a lawyer who can't make it in private practice. He'd lose too much face to show interest in that."

"What? He dissed me like that?"

"Yeah."

"And you're only mentioning it now?"

"Yeah, thought I'd tell you now, because I worry you're starting to like him too much."

I stop him by grabbing his arm and turning him to face me. He's got that silly grin that tells me he's teasing. I reach my arms around him for a hug. His hands drop to my hips and he pulls me up tight against him for a lingering, passionate kiss.

A man down on the wharf yells, "Get a room, you two!"

Nullah releases me, looks around, grins and lifts a hand in acknowledgement, calling out, "Hey, Benson! You jealous?"

He takes my hand and we continue through the parking lot to his truck. As we're driving away, he says, "By the way, that fart story? I guess you came up with that because of Carly's reaction when she saw the look on his face, watching you through the window. But a story about you farting? That was the best you could do? Maybe you could've said it was that joke you like to tell about the penguins going to the zoo. Or Tarzan and his penis transplant."

"I, er, it was just the first thing that came to me. My old jokes aren't funny enough we'd laugh our heads off and Carly's heard them a dozen times. Besides, I didn't think of it. I had to come up with something funny in a hurry, and farts are always funny."

"To some people, anyway."

"Naww, everyone thinks farts are funny," I insist. "But you didn't have to add your bit about how long and loud it was. And how stinky."

"I didn't know why you were lying, but I figured I could do my bit."

"You're a lot more devious than I thought, and very quick on the uptake."

"Chili-scented farts, eh?"

"Want me to prove it?"

"No, I'll take your word for it. I'm going to be sure to be out of range if you ever have to bend over to get your croc out from under the step, though."

I study his strong jaw, the bulk of his bicep, the muscular thigh in his jeans. He glances my way, sees me devouring him with my eyes, and grins. I feel a stirring and wonder how long my desire—no, my unquenchable need—for this man will last. Forever, I hope. But I know that's unrealistic. Even if it doesn't, I'm beginning to think I might still love him once the shine wears off.

Sixteen

Carly

Derek has been super nice all week. He's spent time with me, even helped clearing the table after dinner once. I think he just did that so he could tell me what he wants me to say to Lita at lunch, for the tenth time. He's ready to leave for work now, but comes into the kitchen where I'm clearing away breakfast things, to go over it all again.

"Be sure and tell her I had to take eight courses before I could even article in Canada."

"She was there when you told Nullah that."

"I know!" he snaps. "Tell her again."

"I will."

"And tell her Jackson, Lambert and Duffy had their choice of articling students and chose me."

"Yes."

"And mention I was instrumental in the successful IMF Mills takeover last year."

"I haven't forgotten."

"And remember, there's no other lawyer in town... No, on Vancouver Island and probably not even in Vancouver, that had to take all those courses or that could've aced them like I did."

"Derek, you told me all this just last night." I take a quick breath. Did I actually say that out loud? I must have, because a frown crosses his face and he clenches a fist. I shrink away from him. Is he going to hit me when I'm meeting Lita for lunch in a couple of hours?

Apparently he's decided being nice is a better approach. The black look melts away and he comes to pull me into his arms for one of the nicest ever hugs. Gentle. Snuggly. When he releases me, he cups my shoulders and gives them a quick massage.

"I know I'm making a big thing of this, honey," he says, "but it's really important to me. To us! To our future! You know that bastard Duffy got credit for the last big account that came in, after I did all the grunt work setting it up."

"I know."

"Be sure and tell her that, too. Those bastards let me do all the dog's work and never give me credit. They haven't even been assigning the new work that comes in fairly. I've got bills to pay and a family to support, too. Do they think of that? No. They yammer on about billable hours. The other guys log more billable hours. Well, yeah! Assign me more of the new work coming in, then."

I nod. I've heard all these complaints many times before, but until now, I've never realized how whiny he sounds. I've never noticed his weak chin before, either.

"Don't you dare tell them that last bit! That's between you and me."

"Of course."

He pulls his wallet out of his pocket, opens it, and digs out several bills. "Here," he says, tossing the money on the counter. "Don't use your debit card. Be sure and leave a generous tip and make sure Lita sees that you do." His eyes are so intense I have to look away. "Actually, better yet, pay for her lunch, too." He adds more bills to the pile. "That's more than enough, Carly, but don't think you can keep the change. Be sure to keep the bill. I'll want to see it. Okay?"

"Okay," I agree.

"Call me right after lunch. Okay?"

"Okay," I agree.

He heads to the door, opens it, and turns back to say, "If you screw this up, Carly, you won't be happy." He steps out and pulls the door closed behind him.

I heave a sigh. I won't be happy even if I don't screw it up. It's been months since I was happy. I realize despite my mental pep talks about how lucky I am, it's actually been years. But that's not what he means.

I toy with the money he left, pick it up and count it, calculating there likely won't be more than a few dollars after I pay for two lunches with drinks and a tip. Buying lunch is an asinine, show-off thing to do. Lita and I always went Dutch. It won't feel right: me, acting like a big shot when I don't even have a job, to impress my friend who not only has a job, but a steady, good-paying one. A cloud of hopelessness settles over me.

I pour myself another cup of coffee and collapse onto a chair at the table even though there are still breakfast things to be put away. He's counting on me? Does he really think I can deliver the retainer for him because of a friendship he torpedoed only a short while ago? Does Lita really have that much sway with Nullah and Finn, their company? And if she does, is it even remotely possible she would endorse Derek, someone she called manipulative and a pig, and whom she said she could barely tolerate? No. If they don't choose Derek, will he blame the failure on me? Yes. It will make putting the socks in the wrong area of the drawer seem like a minor failing. No obvious marks, but there was blood in my urine for weeks after that.

Maybe if I told Lita that Derek will blame me if Nullah's company doesn't give him the retainer. I know what she'd say: *He blames you? So what? He'll get over it.* Maybe if I told her I'd get a beating if he blamed me…

I can't do that. She'd never put up with that, wouldn't understand it, and would realize what a total failure I am.

I squeeze my eyes shut and try to fend off the enveloping sense of doom. I wonder if I should go and get Jennifer out of school, and run.

But where would I go? I wouldn't get far in a cab. I have no money and no credit cards. I have a debit card but it's only good for the grocery account. Since my pay from the café doesn't go into it anymore, Derek transfers money into it on the first of every month. He's so secretive about our finances I never know what the balance is. He's told me not to spend more than two hundred a week. So even at the first of the month it's probably less than a thousand dollars. Even if he didn't empty that as soon as he knew we were gone, it wouldn't get us very far.

How did it come to this? How did I let it come to this? It developed gradually and I guess I knew it was happening, but I've never really examined my situation or looked at myself through Lita's eyes before.

I have that detective's card hidden away under the lining behind the little mirror in my jewellery box. I could call her. Maybe she could get Jennifer and me into that women's shelter, at least until things could be sorted out with Derek. But Jennifer would phone her dad the minute she had a chance. I think those women's shelters are pretty secure against husbands trying to get in, but if Jennifer wanted to sneak out and meet her dad? She could probably do it. Derek might think I'm oblivious to all the snide little comments about me he and Jennifer have shared, but I'm not. He's deliberately alienated her. I know that. I just haven't known what to do about it. If I call him on it, or call him on anything for that matter, he gets so mad it scares me. Coward that I am, I've quit arguing with him. A mistake, I know, and now it's too late. Separating from him would surely mean losing her, too.

I indulge in a little cry. My baby! If her father was out of the picture, maybe I could get her back. Would shared custody be a possibility? Would he pay child support? The law says he'd have to, and I've heard they have a number of ways of enforcing it such as attaching bank accounts, but it can take months. How would we live in the meantime?

Would he leave or would I have to go, out of this house? Where would I go? How would I live? I could get back on at the café, or if not that one, another one like it, but pretty tough to live on a minimum wage. I could renew my insurance broker's licence pretty quickly, but even so, I'd be starting at the bottom again in a historically low-paying industry. If I left, I'd be entitled to half the value of the house, though. No, that's not right. It would be half the equity in the house. That can't be much, since we bought it with a high-ratio mortgage and such a big chunk of each payment doesn't reduce the principal but only goes against interest.

If he left and I got the house, the payments, even before he puts a second mortgage on it to buy that stupid boat, would be crippling. Although... What if I could convince him not to buy the boat? And we've been paying on the house for ten years. I think the interest rate went down at the end of the last five-year term. How much are the payments now, anyway? Could I afford it if I rented out the basement? Or rented out the upstairs and moved into the basement myself? It already has a bathroom, a bar sink and doors out to the backyard. It could easily be made into a suite. I bet I could rent a basement suite for half the mortgage payment. Even more if I rented the upstairs. I need to know how much the payments are. The mortgage documents are in Derek's desk. Is there any chance he didn't lock the door today?

I swig the last of my coffee, put the mug in the dishwasher, and go to Derek's study. No luck. The door is locked, as I expected. If there's a key other than the one on his keyring, I don't know where it is. He said the reason he put this lock on the study was to keep toddler Jennifer from messing with his things, but she hasn't cared about going into his study for a few years now and he still keeps it locked. I'm not enough of a dummy to think it's Jennifer he wants to keep out.

I'll have to find a way to ask him what the payments are. It's risky asking him anything about our finances, but I might be able to work a question in when he's talking about that boat, especially if I use it as an argument against taking on more debt. If he'll even discuss it with me.

I go back in the kitchen and finish cleaning up. The compost bin is full, so I take it out to the compost heap behind the garage and empty it. As I'm coming back toward the house, I notice the window to Derek's study is open. It's supposed to rain today, and this is the weather side of the house. If the wind comes up, rain will blow in. Not a good day for him to forget to close the window.

I put the compost bin down and drag one of the Adirondack chairs across the patio to stand on. I take the screen off and lean it against the house. I'm about to slide the window shut when I stop myself. The window is big enough a person could fit through. I think for a moment. What if I could get through? Derek would kill me if he found out. I abandon it as a bad idea, slide the window shut, and get down off the chair.

As I slide the chair back to its usual position, I realize finding out about the mortgage is something I need to do, and getting into his office is probably the only way to do that. Is through the window my only alternative? He would never have to know.

I look up at the window again. Did it latch when I slid it shut? I tow the chair back under the window, climb up on it and push on the metal frame. It slides.

My heart thumps. If I stop now, I'm still okay. I can still say I was just trying to close the window so the rain couldn't get in. I push the window shut. Then I wonder, when will I have another chance? I push the window open as far as it can go.

If he finds out...

I'll just have to make sure he doesn't find out. In and out, five minutes and gone. Ten at the most.

Heart pounding, I put my hands on the sill and hoist my upper body over. I'm halfway in. Is this as far as I can go? It wouldn't be so difficult if I'd ever been good at sports or anything physical, but as the sill digs painfully into my muffin, my biggest regret is the extra pounds I've packed on. I'll have to somersault from here and there's a risk I'll break something in the process. Still, I've come this far. I have to try.

I work my way by pushing my toes up the stucco until only my legs are outside. The hard edges of the sill dig painfully into the least fleshy part of me at the top of my thighs. I'm tempted to back out. But then I give another little push with my toes and now I can put my hands on the credenza. I realize it's not all that different than Downward Dog. I'm surprised by the thought that although I didn't like it much back in the day, I'd like to start going to yoga again. What a crazy random thought to have at a time like this!

I crawl forward, get my knees up on the sill, and then one foot up on it. Now I'm practically doing a handstand. I lose my balance when my hand slips; my elbows collapse, and my face comes perilously close to hitting the credenza. I recover, and hold still until the scream in my head quiets. A bruise on my face could be explained away by clumsiness, but if I fall and break something that makes it impossible for me to move, the injury would be the least of my worries.

I reach back, grab the window frame to pull myself upright and tug on my knee to get it to bend enough so it fits through the window so I'm astraddle the window sill. I bring my trailing leg up, slide my bum, and just like that, I'm standing on the credenza. I carefully climb down. I've left a partial shoe print. I clean it off with my sleeve.

I'm surprised to see Derek didn't take his laptop with him. It's on the desk. I have a momentary urge to see if I can log in, but the niggling fear that Derek might come home unexpectedly has my insides quivering. I tell myself he has no reason to. But what if he does? What if he remembers he left the window open and comes home to close it? He couldn't phone me and ask me to close it since I'm locked out of this room. Maybe he'd tell me where the spare key is so I could get in and save him a trip? *Don't be crazy, Carly! focus on your mission and get out!*

I can't allow myself to get sidetracked. I open the file drawer. Not surprisingly, all the files are in alphabetical order and the one labeled "Mortgage" is near the back of the drawer. I pull it out, lay it on the desk and open it. It's a thin file, containing just the title to the property, the original mortgage document and correspondence about the second term, interest rates and so on. The page I'm looking for is on the back of the third sheet. As I thought, the payments are substantial. I couldn't afford to keep the house even if I could get a loan to pay Derek out.

And then I notice a document titled Canada Life Mortgage Insurance. I scan it quickly, then study-read. I'm surprised he's kept the insurance in force. I feel my pulse quicken as excitement surges through me. If either of us dies, the insurance covers the mortgage.

What am I thinking? He's not going to die. He's only forty, fit, and a non-smoker. An intense stab of regret that he's not terminally ill followed by guilt for wishing him dead washes over me. I put everything back in the file and slide the file back and close the drawer.

Out of curiosity, I open the rest of the drawers. The one over the kneehole is a keyboard tray, so nothing there. As you'd expect, the other drawers contain an assortment of pens and clips and rulers. Extra thumb drives. Cough candies. Breath mints. A stash of chocolate bars. I think nothing of the Altoids tin until I move it, and it rattles. That's not the "curiously strong mints" the label claims it holds, so I open it to find an assortment of keys. A small one that's likely for the locking drawers on the desk and the credenza. One for the cashbox in the left-hand drawer. One big enough to be a house key. Could it be the key to the study?

I go to the door and try it, almost dissolving in happy tears when it works. I slip it into my pocket, go back to the desk and close the Altoids tin and everything else. I remember to close the window, leaving a gap just as Derek had left it. It's his own damn fault if rain comes in and ruins the papers on the credenza. In fact, I kind of like the idea. I leave the room, pull the door shut and lock it. I jiggle the knob to check it just to be sure and go back to the kitchen.

I leave the rest of the breakfast mess and go upstairs to shower and get ready to go to meet Lita for lunch. I'm in a hurry now because I wasted time on the quest for the mortgage documents and I need to take the key somewhere to have a duplicate made before lunch.

Then I think, why bother? Just so I can get into his study anytime I want to? For what? Well, I'm curious about his other files. I didn't even open the credenza. And then there's that cash box. What if he's got lots of money in there?

But I'd never dare steal any of his money and I've got no way of spending it anyway. But I could invade his privacy at will. I would have a secret. Is that worth the bother of getting a duplicate key made?

Yes. I'm going to do it, even though I've already found what I went in for. Even though I'll never get the house. Even if Derek left, he'd want to be paid out for his share and I couldn't manage that. The house would have to be sold. Property values have gone up since we bought it, but starting with just five percent down, there still isn't much equity. Splitting it in half wouldn't result in me getting much of a settlement. But there's that mortgage insurance...

It would be better if he died.

I must be a very bad person, but I can't stop myself from fantasizing about that. Maybe he could be killed in a car accident. Maybe from cancer. Or a heart attack! His father died young. Maybe he will, too. Maybe in ten or fifteen years, the house will be mortgage-free and all mine.

I might not want to keep the house. It would be more convenient to live in town, maybe in a condo development like the one Lita lives in. I could sell the house and buy one of those, and have money left over. I'd be well set up. There would be no more bird houses inside or out, no messy bird feeder, no sorting socks or ironing boxer shorts. No more bruises. It would be hard on Jennifer for a while, but she'll be out on her own by then.

I'll get a job. Maybe in an insurance agency again. Or maybe I'll take a few self-improvement courses. I could even remarry. No, not that. Between living at home, living with Lita, and living with Derek, I've never been on my own. Living alone sounds blissful.

I close my eyes and think, wow, Carly! You climbed in through the window. Found the mortgage and insurance papers. And you're even going to get that key copied. Super Sleuth Carly! You can go in there whenever you want. Check out what else he's hiding. Big deal.

But it is a big deal because even just thinking about doing something so devious—so daring and dangerous!—makes me feel as though my future holds promise. And when I think about even just ten more years with Derek, I realize what Lita meant when she said there are worse things than being alone.

Seventeen

Lita

I arrive at the Lighthouse Bistro a few minutes after twelve to find Carly already at a table by a window overlooking the harbour. She spots me, smiles, and gives a little wave.

"Hey, Carly!" I say as I slide into the chair across from her and nod at her half-empty wineglass. "How are you?"

"Good," she says. But she only looks at me for a heartbeat before looking away.

"Looks like you've been here a while," I comment, with a nod at her wineglass.

"Not too long. You know I hate being late."

"I'm not sure how you put up with me always being late, back in the day."

"It wasn't easy," she says, but she was always so easy going, I know it didn't bug her too much. Or at least she never said anything. She sips her wine, adding another red lipstick print to the rim of the glass.

The server comes to ask if I saw the specials on the signboard at the entrance and know what I want, or if I'd like a few minutes before ordering lunch.

"I'll look at the menu," I tell her as I take the menu card she's handing me.

"Can I get you a drink in the meantime?"

"I'll have a coffee, black, please."

When the server leaves, I tell Carly, "I'm sorry, but I have to go back to work. So no wine for me, but you can get totally blotto if you want. Oh! I guess you're driving."

"No. I came in a cab."

"You still don't have a car?"

"No need," she says, and looks off out the window. I turn my head to see what's drawn her attention, but all I see is raindrops sliding down the glass and a couple of geese bobbing along beside a sailboat tied up at the wharf.

"But it must cost a fortune to take a cab all the way to your place."

"Still more cost effective than buying a second vehicle," she says.

"I guess so," I agree. I can't imagine not being able to get in a car and go where you want, when you want. Why does she go along with it? I realize I haven't seen much of her over the past few years, but should I have seen the change that's come over her? Maybe I did, and maybe it wasn't just Derek I didn't like. We don't seem to have much in common anymore. Is a couple of years spent as roommates when we were hardly more than kids enough to cement a life-long friendship?

I spend a couple of minutes on the menu and ask Carly what she's decided on.

"I'm going to have the fish and chips."

"Again? Twice in one week?"

"Well, it's different here. They do it with salmon instead of cod or halibut."

"Hmm," I shrug. Okay, I guess. When the server comes with my coffee, I decide I could have one glass of wine, and order a glass of house white along with a vegetarian quesadilla. While we're waiting for our food, I break the awkward silence by asking what she's done all week.

"Oh, you know, there's lots of stuff to do."

"Like what? You haven't put anything on Facebook or Instagram for so long I've totally lost track of what you're interested in these days."

"I'm not on social media anymore."

"Oh? Why not?"

"Too much of a time suck."

"I guess it can be," I agree. "I spend about an hour a day. Mostly in the evening, when I'm watching TV. So, what do you do for fun? I know you talked about quilting."

"I gave that up."

"Oh? How come?"

"What's the point of making a bunch of useless quilts?"

"But even if you don't want them yourself, people sell them, for big money. And what about wall hangings? Some of them are really beautiful. With your arts background—"

"Yeah, my useless education."

"But Carly! You're really gifted! Now that Jennifer's in school all day, you could take a graphic arts course and maybe even start your own business. Online, even."

"I don't know. I'm not like you, Lita. I don't have a head for business. Besides, I wouldn't have time."

Why is she so apathetic? I study the pretty woman across the table from me and realize she's a stranger. Finally she breaks the silence by saying, "You know, Derek is a really good lawyer. He would really be a good choice for Nullah's business."

Okay, now I know what's going on. The only reason she's here is to promote her asshole husband. I catch my lower lip in my teeth to stop myself from saying something I might regret.

"He was really instrumental in that pulp mill merger a couple of years ago," she continues. "He does more work than any of the other guys and they often come to him when they can't figure something out."

She looks so earnest, I don't know what to say. The server brings our food, so I'm saved from having to respond. I pick at my salad, decide to put the dressing on it after all, and drizzle the raspberry vinaigrette over the leaves. I realize if she really does nothing but look after the house, she's become so uninteresting I don't want to know what's going on in her life. How much discussion about what cleaner is best for marble countertops or how far apart to hang your husband's shirts can I tolerate? If Derek is an abuser, I can't save her. I'm not certain she's being abused, anyway. It might just be that she loves her husband being a take-charge kind of guy, so it's not necessarily all on Derek. You can't be a doormat if you don't lie down.

I take a bite of quesadilla followed by a long swallow of my wine and decide that as soon as I've eaten half my lunch, I'm leaving.

"You know, Derek aced those exams—"

I can't stop myself from thumping the table with the flat of my hand. "For the love of god, Carly," I hiss. "I didn't want to have lunch with you so we could talk about Derek."

She looks so stricken, I regret my outburst. Until she babbles on: "But he'd be the best fit for Nullah's company. That's why he was short-listed."

"Carly," I say more gently, "Derek is a chump, always bragging, always patting himself on the back, always running everyone else down. I see it. Nullah and Finn see it. And I think if you were honest with yourself, you'd see it too. They don't like him! Abbo Fitness is *not* going to put him on retainer."

"Oh," she moans. She puts her fork down suddenly and nearly collapses against the back of her chair. Her face works and she seems to be struggling to keep her composure.

I'd like to be sympathetic but instead of summoning empathy, her snivelling disgusts me. "I have to use the ladies' room," I say. I get up and wend my way through tables to the washroom. On my way back, I stop at the cashier desk and pay the bill.

I come back to the table, sit down again, and finish my wine in one long swallow. "I have to go. Stay and finish your lunch. I paid the bill."

If I thought she was struggling to keep her composure before, now she looks downright terrified. "No! Oh, no!" She brings her hands up to cover her face and I hear a little squeak as if she's stifling sobs. A couple at the next table look over curiously.

After a moment, I say, "Carly? What's going on?"

She takes her hands off her face and looks at me. "You can't pay the bill. I have to pay the bill."

"Why?"

"Derek told me to pay for lunch."

"Well, just tell him I got to it first."

"He won't understand." She chokes back a sob and wails, "You don't know! He just won't understand!"

Now there are other diners watching. I reach across and take her hand. "Come on, Carly," I say, "let's get out of here."

I get up and pull her to her feet, then herd her out the door, down the gangway and onto the seawall. It's raining heavily enough it's a lousy day for a walk, but there are still a few hardy pedestrians. When two women under umbrellas are past us and there's no one else close, I ask, "What's this all about?"

She just shakes her head and looks at the ground in front of her.

"What happens if he doesn't understand?" I press. "What? Does he hurt you?"

She still can't make eye contact, but at least she nods.

I pull her to a stop and put my arms around her. She breaks into full-throated sobbing. I wait until she's calmed, and say, "My god, Carly! I'm so sorry! How long has this been going on?"

"Th-th-the first time was when Jennifer was about two." She draws a breath and looks at me, then begins speaking hysterically, as if the floodgates were opened. "She got into his study and used a black sharpie on some papers he had on his desk, as well as on her arms and his leather chair. It was my fault. Kids can be so quick! I only looked away for a couple of minutes. She was playing on the family room floor and when I next looked, she wasn't. I wasn't watching her carefully enough, he said. Bad enough she ruined what he had spent a lot of time on as well as the chair, but besides that, she could've gotten hurt. He slapped me."

"But he slapped you again after that? He's kept slapping you?"

"Worse than that," she sobs. "He's always sorry after. He always says he lost control and it'll never happen again." Her nose is running. I dig a Kleenex out of my purse and hand it to her. She honks into it and stuffs it in her pocket before continuing: "Of course it does happen again."

"There is help, Carly. You can get help."

She stiffens and says sharply, "Yeah, I know." She draws herself up, takes a deep breath, and says, "But there's nothing they can do that will stop him from taking Jennifer away from me if I leave him."

"But there is!"

"No, there isn't! She's big enough now. She would find a way to get with him. She loves him more than she loves me. A lot more. He's already told me he would take her to his mother's place in Phoenix and I'd never see her again."

"But he moved here to get away from his mother, remember? I don't think he'd go there. And anyway, he can't do that. The cops in Phoenix would go and get her. You'd get custody. You're a good mom, no judge would give him custody—"

"No!" Her mascara is running in streaks. I can't tell if it's because of the rain, which is drenching both of us, or if she's still crying. "He didn't come here to get away from his mother, he came here to meet someone he'd been chatting with on line. And then she turned out to be too needy so he dumped her but he liked it here and decided to stay."

"Oh, okay, but—"

"He'd just take her. Jennifer. He wouldn't wait for some judge to give me custody. And how would the cops find her? I don't know his mother's name, much less her address."

"It's not Wilton? And in all the time you've been married, you've never been there?"

"She remarried. And no, I haven't been there. He thought it was important to reconnect with his mother, so he's taken Jennifer to visit a few times. But I've never gone with them."

"He took Jennifer and left you at home?"

"He said it was for my own good. It would be awkward because his mother wouldn't like me, but Jennifer should get to know her grandmother. It's better if I'd stay home to take care of things."

"I don't know about that, but why wouldn't she like you?"

"Well, she was a yoga instructor. She'd hate me because she's very careful about her weight and I'm fat."

I seriously doubt Carly being Rubenesque would be something Derek's mother couldn't overlook for a weekend. What would she do, anyway? Refuse to let her in the house? Make fun of her? That's crazy. But Derek comments on her weight so often he's got Carly convinced she's fat. Why did he marry her? It's not like she was skinny when they met. And it's a lame excuse. But I don't belabour the point.

"You're not fat, Carly, you've just got curves in the right places. And you used to go to yoga. You'd have something in common with his mother. But it doesn't matter." I feel rain running down my face and wipe my hand across my forehead to clear it. "But you—he's going to be mad at you? Hurt you because Nullah's company isn't going to use him?"

She nods.

"What if that changed?"

"There would be something else," she says, and exhales loudly. "Maybe not for a while, but there's always something else."

"But it would keep you safe for long enough for you to see a lawyer, or pack a few things and move out, to safety. You have to do something before he really hurts you. You could move into my condo. I'm living with Nullah now, you know, my condo's empty anyway. I'll give you the key." I dig into my purse, get my key ring, and start to work the condo key off. "This is for the back door, you know, around the side—"

"Never mind, Lita. I can't go there. He knows where you live, he'd be sure and check it out and he'd find me. I know you mean well. But I shouldn't have told you. Please don't let on that I told you. Please, please, *please* don't tell anyone! It would only make it worse. This is my problem. *My* problem. Even if Nullah puts him on retainer, something else will come along. I realize that now." She turns back and hurries away.

"Carly, wait!" I call after her. "Come to Nullah's instead, then. We'll help you! We'll go pick up Jennifer and make sure he can't get her!"

But she doesn't stop, just lifts a hand in a kind of wave and walks faster, heading for the cab stand at the Harbour Air office.

"Call me! Anytime!" I yell this loudly enough that people going up the steps up to Front Street turn around to look.

I hurry back under the canopy on the gangway to get out of the rain, pull out my phone and call Nullah. Carly asked me not to tell anyone about the abuse, but I tell Nullah anyway. He agrees to call Derek and tell him they won't be hiring a local lawyer after all because they've decided to go with someone in-house. He'll also phone the managing partner of Jackson, Lambert and Duffy and sing Derek's praises, assuring him it was a tough decision. They were impressed with Derek and would've retained him if they hadn't decided to add another lawyer to their in-house team instead, and so on.

"Tell the senior partner to be sure he lets Derek Fucking Wilton know how much you and Finn liked him. I know it's asking a lot but maybe you can find something positive to say about him. You like his shoes, or something."

"I'll try," Nullah agrees. I almost grin imagining Nullah telling the senior partner he liked a lawyer because of his nice shoes. It might be funny if it wasn't so serious.

Hopefully that's enough to save Carly a beating. I don't know what else to do. I realize it was a big step, her telling me about it. If it keeps her safe for the time being—if she has a little more time—maybe she'll find the strength to do something about it.

Eighteen

Carly

As soon as I get home, I return the original key to the Altoids box in Derek's desk. I look at his laptop and wonder if I can use it. If there isn't a password, maybe. Do I dare? Just for a minute, because Jennifer is due home soon. I stroke it, then quickly open it. There's no password request. The screen flashes on.

It's not a legal document or any kind of work thing, though, it's a video. I click the start arrow and gasp when I realize what I'm looking at: a bruised and bloodied woman, naked, shackled to a pipe in a dingy basement. There's a man with his back to the camera, viewed from shoulders to knees, a folded belt in his hand. As he raises it, I slam the laptop shut and race out of the study, making sure to lock the door behind me.

When my new duplicate key is safely concealed with the detective's card behind the lining in my jewelry box, I come back to the kitchen and put the money on counter where Derek will see it as soon as he comes in. No use avoiding the inevitable.

Jennifer comes home and dumps her wet backpack on the floor. "Don't leave that there," I tell her.

"I won't," she agrees, and goes to the pantry, shuffles through the cookies and granola bars and comes out with one of each before heading up to her room. She likely won't be down again before Derek comes home, and the backpack on the floor will be in the way when he comes in. I go and hang it on a hook in the mudroom.

I'm making pork chops for dinner and get the frying pan out. Derek will be home before I know it. I'm planning to brown the chops and pour a can of mushroom soup over them. Tasty, but a little slap-dash. I decide to pound them flat and bread them instead. No longer pork chops, but pork schnitzel, definitely up a couple of notches. Derek loves schnitzel. Maybe it will make up for my failure at lunch.

As I work, that few seconds of video I saw keeps replaying in my brain. I try to stop it, but can't. Try to quit worrying about how Derek will react when he learns I didn't pay for lunch and can't do that either. He's never used his belt on me but now that he's seen it in that video, will today be the first time? Maybe he'll be satisfied if I explain she paid without me knowing. Or better, that she said Nullah wanted her to pay. A gesture of respect?

I cut the meat off the bone, dig the meat tenderizer hammer out of the drawer and start to work on the first chop. Before I realize it, I'm hitting it harder, faster, and screaming as I do it, then stop, dissolving into tears and collapsing to the floor. Did I actually scream? Did Jennifer hear me?

I lean back against the cabinets, collect myself, and wipe my eyes on my sleeve as I study the little hammer. Smooth on one side of the head, a grid pattern of sharp bumps, bits of meat still clinging to them, on the other. Funny, although I've had it for years, I've never realized what a nice heft it has in my hand.

I remind myself time is passing, and besides, I don't want Jennifer to come down and find me like this. I stand up and get back to work on the chops. The one I was pounding before my little meltdown resembles ground pork and has a hole the size of a quarter. Even the cutting board underneath has holes in it. I start crying again, then tell myself to smarten up. Derek will be home soon. Crying is enough to send him off the deep end any time and he'll be mad I didn't pay for lunch, so I don't want him to find me blubbering like a baby on top of that. I close the hole in the schnitzel by squishing it back together. It'll be fine once it's floured, egged and breaded. I set it on the plate next to the bowl of panko crumbs, and start on the next one.

As I pound, I get a fleeting mind image of the little hammer smashing into Derek's head. My god! Where did that come from? I should be disgusted at the thought, but it's oddly satisfying. I fantasize Derek coming into the kitchen, seeing the money, and winding up to punch me in the stomach. I yell: *she paid before we even got the bill!* I swing the hammer. It connects with his head with a meaty *thunk* as if it's a pork cutlet. He topples over. I'm appalled I would even have such a fantasy, and hiss, "Stop it, Carly!"

But the fantasy comes right back, different this time. Now he has thrown a dish of Cherries Jubilee off the dining room table and is telling me to clean it up. *Thunk!* The meat tenderizer connects with his forehead. Why was the little hammer in the dining room? It must have been in my pocket. No, my yoga pants don't have pockets. Am I in jeans? Not likely. Derek says women like me, with big butts, don't look good in jeans, so I haven't bought any since I outgrew the last pair about five years ago. Anyway, I wouldn't put the hammer in my pocket. I must have had time to run out to the kitchen and get it, come running back in brandishing it over my head and yell *clean it up yourself! Thunk!* He's on the floor and I'm leaning over him, unmoved by the mind picture of his eyes staring sightlessly at the ceiling and blood running from the neat pattern of holes in his forehead. Is that his skull showing through? Blood runs off his face and drips onto the carpet. That's going to be hard to get out. I replay the whole fantasy, but now it's in the kitchen, and I've used the smooth side. Like Maxwell's Silver Hammer. The Beatles' song floods my brain as I try to push the image out of my head. It keeps coming back, along with what I remember of the lyrics. Like Maxwell, I'll make sure he is dead. Is it really that easy to kill someone?

I still get a queasy little jiggle in my insides when I think how I broke into Derek's study. That was quite a feat for a fat woman, and I'm proud I could do it. And getting that duplicate key cut! And sneaking a look at Derek's computer, much as I regret seeing what I saw.

I've had quite a day. It's a brand-new Carly. No, not new, just someone who was dead for a while and has been resurrected at last.

Why did discovering Derek has been in there, not working as he always says he is but watching violent porn, have such an impact on me? I know guys like porn a lot more than women do, and according to a magazine article I once read, just because they watch it doesn't mean there's anything wrong with their real life relationship. But watching a helpless woman being brutalized is beyond healthy, isn't it? I would never in a million years have dreamed Derek would watch porn at all, let alone something that hideous. Then I wonder why I'm surprised.

I wish I hadn't turned into a blubbering mess at lunch, though. What must Lita think of me? She's probably disgusted. No way would she ever put up with a man beating her. But I did have the courage to stand up to her. Tell her it's my problem and I don't need her help. I don't need anyone's help.

Oddly, admitting what was going on in my life—that I was wrong about Derek—wasn't as difficult as I thought it would be. Maybe because Lita has been a friend for so long. We knew all each other's secrets back then. I'm beginning to feel kind of proud that I told her.

Jennifer comes downstairs and into the kitchen. "I'm hungry," she says.

"You know we don't eat until your father gets home."

"I can't wait that long."

"You had a snack, didn't you?"

"Yeah, a granola bar. But I'm still hungry. I'll have French fries now."

"Don't be silly, Jennifer, I'm not going to make French fries for you now. You're a big girl. Your father will be home in an hour or so. Go do your homework. You can wait." I count as a small victory the expression of surprise that flickers across her face before the frown returns.

"You're mean! I hate you!" she shrieks. "I'll be glad when you're gone!"

"I'm not going anywhere and you watch your mouth, little girl, or you won't get any dinner at all!"

I hear her thumping up the stairs and then her door slams. She's probably going to pout and I'll have to coax her to come down for dinner. Then I realize she can stay there. I'm done coaxing her to do anything. Today, I broke two cardinal rules: I broke into the Forbidden Study, and I told Lita about being abused. It's just the beginning.

I'm a young Miss Marple! No. Miss Marple wasn't married. More like Alex Morrow. She has a husband and kids. Alex Morrow wouldn't put up with her kids treating her like Jennifer treats me and I'm not going to put up with that any longer, either. My god! I stood up to a ten-year-old. Whoop-de-do.

Then I think about what she said: *I'll be glad when you're gone.* What ten-year-old thinks like that? Where would she even get the idea? Is it something Derek talks about? Sure, he tells me he'll take me for a boat ride and I won't come back, but it's an idle threat, a figure of speech like when Ariana says her boyfriend would kill her if she damaged his car when she borrowed it. Surely he wouldn't tell Jennifer I'm going away. What kid wants to lose their mother?

New resolve floods through me. I'm not going anywhere, at least not without her, and she can stay up there all night if she wants to. I won't beg her to come down. I find myself smiling as I peel potatoes, cut them into fries, and put them in ice water in the sink. When Derek gets home I'll pat them dry, ready for the deep fryer.

I'm putting the peels in the compost bin when I realize it was when I emptied it that I saw the study window slightly open and got the idea of going through it. And that I forgot about putting the screen back up. If Derek sees that—! I dry my hands and hurry out the back door, but before I get around the corner, Derek drives in and parks. He's home early. Will he notice the screen?

He slides out of the driver's seat, shuts the door, and comes around the back of the vehicle. "Hey," he says, "you were supposed to phone me right after lunch."

"My phone died."

"How many times do I have to tell you, you need to be better about making sure you charge it? I don't like trying to call repeatedly and getting nothing."

"I know. I'm sorry. I was just kind of distracted, getting ready to go for lunch. Trying to remember everything you told me to say, so I wouldn't forget anything."

He gives a sort of half-nod. The excuse is acceptable. I'm a half-wit, after all. He glances at the patio; his gaze falls on the Adirondack chair where it's not supposed to be and the screen propped against the house.

"What's going on there?" he asks. "Did you do that?"

My guts clench. "I, er, yeah, I was going to take all the screens down. You know, for the winter. And I ran out of time."

"Why would you want to take the screens down?"

"It's just that I was, um, looking out the kitchen window and thought, that screen is dirty, I should take it down and clean it. And I might as well do all of them. And then I thought maybe they could be put away for the winter."

He lifts a hand to silence me. "So you started on that one and left it at that?"

"Yeah, I, uh, shouldn't have started it when I knew I'd have to leave..."

"Get that put away. It looks like someone was trying to break in. And why the fuck didn't you close the window while you were at it?"

"I thought you wanted it open," I say, exhaling a long breath I didn't know I was holding. "I'll finish up with the screens first thing tomorrow."

I open the door for him to go into the house ahead of me and follow him inside. He goes straight to his study to put his briefcase away.

I hold my breath. Did I leave any evidence that I was in there? Any tell-tale signs like something out of place? I wiped the footprint off the credenza, but where there others I didn't notice?

When he doesn't come roaring out in a rage, I breathe easily again. Then I hear his footsteps going up the stairs. When he comes back down and into the kitchen, he's in sweatpants and T-shirt. He gets a beer out of the fridge.

"Jenny in her room?" he asks.

"Yes. I wasn't planning to have dinner ready before five, but I can move it up now. Fifteen minutes?"

"Sure," he says, but instead of going through to the family room to watch TV until dinner, he pulls up a stool on the far side of the peninsula and sits there watching me work. I turn the deep fryer on and get the French fries patted dry and put in the basket, ready to go into the oil when it's hot enough. I turn to breading the meat. I feel his eyes on my back. My hands shake and the first schnitzel slips into the pan with a splash. Drops of the hot oil hit my wrist. I bite my tongue and don't let on that it hurt.

Finally, Derek says, "Well? Are you going to tell me?"

"Tell you what?"

"How your lunch went?"

"I couldn't really...I mean, I told her everything you said—"

"You're a piss poor liar, you know," he interrupts. "Your phone wasn't fuckin' dead. You just didn't want to tell me."

"But I—"

"Never mind. I already know they're not going to give me the retainer."

I draw a sharp breath and turn to face him, expecting to see the black thundercloud expression he gets when he's about to explode. Instead, he looks rather pleased with himself. "I also know you didn't pay for lunch like I told you to."

"I, er, you're not mad?"

"No. It's fuckin' awesome, actually. Nelly called me. Nice gesture of respect, not letting you pay! And he said they would have given me the retainer but didn't because they've decided to hire an in-house lawyer. Then Jackson comes into my office and says Nelly called him too, and was very *very* flattering. So my stock with Jackson has definitely gone up. He's decided my charge-out rate is too low as I've been telling him for fuckin' years, and he's going to bump it up by fifty dollars an hour."

"Oh, that's awesome!"

"Yeah! And even better, instead of the firm keeping fifty-five percent of what I bill, effective immediately, this month even, they only keep fifty. So now that loan for my new boat should go sailing right through, no pun intended. And it's thanks to my connection with Nelly."

"Umm, another loan?"

"How did you think I was going to get the new boat? The loans officer has been humming and hawing, yammering about my debt service ratio, their standards, blah blah. I told them I'll give them a collateral mortgage on the house but that wasn't good enough for them. And now my expected earnings going forward will be ten or fifteen percent more. Plenty of cash for my debt service ratio." He drains his beer and says, "This calls for a proper celebration. I'm getting a Chivas. You want one?"

"Um, no thanks." He's asking me if I want a drink? Nullah must really have flattered him. Maybe me, too. But he still wants to buy a new boat? "Well, um, why do you need a new boat now that you know there's, um, no retainer?"

He dismisses my question with a wave of his hand, stands and heads toward the liquor cabinet in the family room. At the top of the stairs he holds up and turns to face me.

"Okay. You don't need to know this, but I'll tell you anyway. I called about the loan as soon as I got the news, and they told me they'll review my new financials next week and should have an answer for me

Thursday or Friday. As soon as I get the boat, I'm going to apply for the in-house position. It means quitting Jackson, Lambert and fucking Duffy, of course, but they can suck my balls. Nelly sang my praises to the moon, Carly! I show up in the new boat and they'll see I'm as well fixed as any of them. Of course, I need the boat sooner rather than later. I thought I'd have to wait until after Christmas, but I'll be able to close the deal before that now. We'll invite Nelly and Lita out for a boat ride. I'll be in a great bargaining position. I don't need them, they need me. The way Nelly praised me, it's a given I'll get the job. I won't take it right away. I'll ask what the benefits are. Is there a pension? How about extended dental and eye care? Jennifer's going to need braces, so I'll make a point of asking if they cover orthodontics."

He takes a few steps toward me, a cat-that-ate-the-canary expression on his face such as I don't think I've ever seen before.

"I'll get a boat that's bigger than fuckin' Nelly's. Imagine *that* tied up to our dock! People will think, wow, the guy that owns that place must be really top shelf. Imagine how everyone will stare when I cruise past the Lighthouse and Miller's Landing and Stone's Marina! Even over to the Dinghy Dock. I'll join the Yacht Club. I'll run for Commodore! Your husband is finally going to get the respect he deserves." He gives a sharp nod as if to make it so, then turns and continues away, his body language reminding me so much of a cartoon clown I almost expect him to leap up and click his heels together.

My heart sinks. I'm stunned. Nullah said nice things about Derek? A new boat? Another drain on our finances, counting on a bigger paycheque and a new job? Does he even know what the in-house job pays? Another lien against the house. We'll be drowning in debt. That may not bother Derek, but it cuts me to the core. I'm counting on my share of the equity in the house to give me a start when I leave him.

When I leave him? I'm actually considering leaving! Will I be able to go through with it? What makes me think I can? Just the fact I climbed through a window, admitted to Lita that he's been beating me all these years, and stood up to my daughter? I must be losing my mind.

But if what I'm feeling is losing my mind, I like it.

Nineteen

Lita

Christmas is fast approaching and I still have no clue what to get for Nullah. What family he has is in Australia. I called his sister, but since she hasn't seen him in more than three years, she doesn't know what he's interested in now, other than me, his boat and his business.

There is really nothing I could buy for either the boat or the business that he doesn't already have. No help there. He only wears a tie once a year, when he goes to Toronto. He has a Smart watch he swears by. He doesn't play video games. He doesn't really have any hobbies other than fishing, and he's got two tackle boxes full of stuff for that. Am I doomed to give him socks for our first Christmas together?

Nullah bought my present a week ago. The damn thing is wrapped and has been sitting on the fireplace mantel taunting me ever since. The box isn't big, but then it's not small, either. I expect it to be jewelry, but the box is more like a watch box, a cube. I, too, have a FitBit so I don't think it's a watch. It doesn't rattle and it's not very heavy.

He did a nice job of wrapping it. This morning, I casually mention how beautifully the gift is wrapped. He admits he had the people at the store wrap it.

"Oh yeah? What store wraps gifts?"

"Nice try," he says. He gives me a quick kiss as I'm heading out the door. "Are you working late tonight?"

"Don't think so. You?"

"Nothing pressing. I should be home at the usual time."

"I've got a conference call this afternoon. Hopefully we can settle it today. In any case, I should be home by five. I'll pick up Chinese on my way home."

"Good. See you at dinner, then."

It's raining, but it's only a dozen steps to the garage so I don't take an umbrella, I just run. As I drive toward town, I notice what might be a few white flakes mixed in with the rain. I wonder if I should've had winter tires put on my car as Nullah suggested weeks ago. I don't own winter tires because my car came with all weathers, all you need on Vancouver Island, or so I thought. Nullah says that's fine for around town but now that I'm living out here where the roads don't get plowed for days or maybe not at all if it rains, not good enough, and I could end up in the ditch. He's going to take my car to his mate with the tire shop and get winter tires put on this weekend. He claims he'll get a good deal and says not to worry about paying. I'm beginning to realize Nullah always has some kind of connection to get a deal.

I settle into my office, open the file in readiness for the conference call, and decide to text Carly. I haven't seen her since lunch at the Lighthouse, but lately we chat on the phone every day at about ten a.m., my usual coffee break time. I'm going to be in a meeting this morning, so I quickly text her to let her know.

It was a shocker to learn from Finn that Derek emailed his CV and an application for the non-existent in-house position. It's unfortunate we didn't think to tell him at the outset that the position was already filled, but then we assumed he'd think the job was beneath him. Now if we say it's been filled, he'll want to know why they didn't offer it to him, in light of those very complimentary phone calls to his bosses. Nullah could say they didn't want to poach him. Would Derek accept that?

Who cares what Derek thinks? I wouldn't, except if he took it as a snub he might blame it on Carly, and we know where it would go from there. They're going to tell him the position is in the Toronto office.

I sigh and lean back in my chair. At least Carly has opened up about Derek abusing her. It must be easier to talk about it over the phone, probably because it's more anonymous. She said one of the worst times was after Finn left their house, which was a couple of weeks before the four of us went for lunch at the Dinghy Dock, and that's how she got the scar under her eye. But that was the last time, and he's been like a changed man since.

The reason he's been so mellow? It's not because he's seen the error of his ways, or got his temper under control. Oh god no, no positive introspection for that cretin. He thinks he's Mr. Wonderful now. That he's a shoo-in for the job. Carly says she has never seen him in such a good mood for such a long time. He even agreed to let her start going to yoga again. Not right away, but maybe in the spring. Ha! The bastard will never let it happen. But for some reason Carly believes him.

I have bouts of regret when I wish I had never agreed to reconnect with Carly. I worry his prolonged cheerful mood will lull her into a false sense of wellbeing, like the bad times are behind her, and she'll think she's safe. Not an unfounded worry, given the yoga thing. Then I have periods of optimism when I think I'll be able to help her. Provide her with the moral support to get rid of the bastard. Whatever the reason, she's more like the old Carly.

I've read the statistics. So many women murdered by their significant others, every month. Even in Canada. Carly hasn't said anything about a separation. I worry that she's dragging her feet because she doesn't believe me when I tell her abusers don't stop abusing, especially now that he's being so nice. I'm afraid she will stay with him until he kills her.

My phone rings and Nullah's face pops up on the screen.

"Hi, babe," he says as soon as I answer.

"Hey! I'm just going to head to a meeting."

"This won't take long. I just wanted to let you know what the slimy little bastard has done."

"Slimy... Derek?"

"Of course, Derek. If he wants that job, he sure has a funny way of ingratiating himself."

"What do you mean?"

"Alvin called me this morning."

"Alvin Benson? From the Yacht Club?"

"Yeah, *Detective* Alvin Benson. You won't believe it. Wilton tipped them off that I was running drugs. Dealing out of the clubs."

"What?"

"Yeah. In his tiny mind, I race down to Mexico in my boat to pick up the goods. Cops have to look into it, of course. Benson already checked with the Harbour Master to confirm the boat has never been gone long enough for a trip like that, but he said they'd like to go over it just so they can show they've done their due diligence, and close the file. I'm going over now to give them the keys."

"Oh my god, Nullah!"

"He actually had the balls to ask about a reward. And he wants to be a C.I."

"Holy shit! I'm sorry. I knew he was a bastard, but I really didn't imagine he could ever come up with anything this bizarre." I glance at my watch and realize I'm late for the meeting. "I can't talk now, baby, but—this won't be a problem for you, will it?"

Hesitation at his end of the line makes my guts clench.

"Will it?" I reiterate.

"No," he says at last. "At least it shouldn't be. But you know, not all my friends are squeaky clean."

I draw a deep breath. "I'm sorry. I'll call you as soon as I get out of the meeting."

"It's okay. Cuzza this, I've got a lot of running around to do today. How about instead of you picking up Chinese, I meet you at The Crow and Gate for dinner?"

"Deal. See you there. Love you."

"Love you."

I touch the end call button and head for the conference room. Focusing on the recent changes in the Enhanced All Risks Homeowner's Policy is not easy, with the news of Derek's latest asshole deed swirling around in my head. And not all Nullah's friends are squeaky clean? I guess if I'm honest, I knew some of them were a little sketchy. The bikers, especially. Everyone's heard stories about them, and not many are about the Christmas Toy Rides.

Derek doesn't realize it, but he may have stirred up a hornet's nest.

Twenty

Carly

The cab stops at the curb in front of London Drugs. I pay the driver in cash.

He says, "What, no chit today?"

"Nope, not today." Naturally I don't tell him Derek checks the invoice from the cab company. He says it's to make sure they don't overcharge him but really, he just wants to know where I go and how long I stay there. I definitely don't want him to know I went to the mall.

"Want me to wait for you?"

"You could do that? But..."

"I don't have the meter running. I'll wait over there," he indicates another Yellow Cab at the edge of the parking lot closest to the casino. "I might get another fare before you're done, but I might not, so when you come out, check to see if I'm still here."

"Thanks! I'll do that," I agree, and head into the store. I know he's only a cab driver, but he's young and good looking and the way he looks at me makes me feel good. I have come to look forward to seeing him and I'm disappointed when it's a different driver. Yeah, I'm that pathetic.

It's been so long since I've been in London Drugs I'm disoriented. Eventually I see what I'm looking for. I look at the display of a dozen tablets, overwhelmed. So this one, in my price range, is a *10.1 inch Android Tablet (Android 5.1 1280 x 800 Quad Core 2GB+32GB) / 64 / Mini USB / SIM Card Slot / TF Card slot / 3.5mm Earphone Jack*. The only part of that I understand is the earphone jack. A sales associate comes along and offers to help. I tell her I was hoping to get an iPad, but they're out of my price range. She assures me this android tablet will do the trick for me. It's internet ready. She shows me how to open the settings, where I'll need to enter our WIFI password, and then accompanies me to the cashier. I refuse the offered plastic bag and rush back outside. I'm in luck. The cab I came in is still waiting.

In less than two hours since leaving, I'm back home. I get my precious new tablet out of the box and all the packaging disposed of—Styrofoam and plastic in their respective recycling bins (Styrofoam broken up into discreet pieces of course)—the box on the burn pile and burned. No one will care about the fire at this time of the year, with everything so wet. I've been cleaning up the yard and piling branches and dead plant stuff there for weeks, so Derek won't think anything of it. I make sure the box is completely destroyed and stir the ashes before I leave the fire to burn down, and go back inside to get a chicken in the oven for dinner. With the oven on, I might as well make peanut butter chocolate chip cookies, Jennifer's favorite. Also, buns and banana bread, which Derek loves. Might as well fill the oven and soften up the husband at the same time. While the cookies bake, I mix and mash bananas and dry rub the chicken.

Thoughts of my tablet, wondering if I'll really be able to get it set up, trying to decide on the best place to hide the owner's manual, distract me from my work and the cookies on the edge of the pan get a little burnt. I pull them out and the banana bread and chicken go in. The buns will have to wait since they haven't risen enough yet.

Jennifer won't eat the cookies with the black on them, so I munch them down while they're still warm. So delicious! I know that's a lot of calories and I ate way too many, but the evidence is destroyed. No one can ridicule me for burning them, and there's no one to witness my gluttony.

I'm not really interested in what I'm doing because I'd so much rather be setting up my tablet. I have the key to his study, of course, so it won't take me long to get in and out, but it might take me a while to find the WIFI password. My iPhone was connected to it but no way I remember the password. The store clerk told me it'll be on the router. I don't know what, or where, that is. She described it for me so I think I'll recognize it when I see it. I don't dare to try for it today. Jennifer gets home shortly after three and I can't risk her catching me at it. Maybe I'm paranoid and maybe I'm being overly cautious, but I don't even trust my own daughter not to rat me out.

Besides the statement from the cab company Derek monitors the bank statements, but he hasn't yet wanted to see the till tapes from the stores. I always make sure to lose the till tapes, but that will have to end if he ever gets interested. I hope that never happens, because I add cash back to each order. The first time, it was just twenty dollars. At dinner that day, I told him I'd been shopping and complained about how groceries have gone up. I shopped again a few days later, another forty dollars. He got a little pissy at me going out so often and suggested I should make a list and get everything I need in one trip. I said I like to have fresh produce, reminding him of his high standards. No marginal romaine for his Caesar salads! That was an argument he could get behind.

I took a real risk the last time and added eighty dollars and nervously waited for the 'not sufficient funds' message to come up. I nearly collapsed when it didn't. Eighty dollars was what I needed to top up the kitty to cover cab fare for the trip, and a tablet. It was enough, just. I gave the last of my money to the cabbie. Generous. And also, it's safer for me not to have to explain why I have cash, in case Derek checks my purse.

At this moment, the tablet is hidden away between the mattress and box spring on my side of the bed. I fantasize about surfing the net again. It's the weekend now, though, so it'll have to wait until Monday.

I see the car come up the driveway. Derek's home early, not unusual on a Friday, and it looks like he picked Jennifer up from school. I hope he won't mind that dinner will be another hour, at least. Maybe he can spend some time on his latest birdhouse or mulling over the specs for his new boat, or get a beer and watch ESPN. He's whistling as he comes in the door. That's odd.

Jennifer enters the kitchen first, screws up her face and says, "I smell smoke. Did you burn something?"

"Um, I guess some of the cookies got a little dark. Just on the bottom."

"Well, it smells like you burned them." She snorts and pokes through the pile of cookies on the plate before scooping up a handful.

"Change out of your uniform before you—" I start.

"Yeah, yeah," she cuts me off, in a near perfect imitation of her father. But at least she heads for the front hall and up the stairs.

"Hi, honey," Derek greets me as he's taking off his jacket. He comes to give me a kiss. That's really odd. I wonder what happened. "How long until dinner's ready?"

"Um, I wasn't expecting you so early. I'm sorry. It'll be another hour at least. Maybe I can make it sooner..."

"That's okay," he says. "I want to catch the highlights from last night's game, anyway." He goes upstairs and comes back down in his sweats, gets a beer and takes it into the family room. In seconds, I hear hockey highlight commentary from the TV.

I wonder what's happened to put him in such a cheerful mood. He was pissed when I told him the in-house position at Abbo Fitness was in Toronto and he's been grouchy ever since. When I hear a commercial come on TV, I go to the doorway to the family room and ask, "Did you have a good day?"

"I did," he replies without looking at me. "I heard from Boatland in Sidney today. I'm getting that boat, Carly. The one that's bigger than Nelly's."

"Oh." My guts clench. "But I thought you didn't need it now that you aren't trying to get that job."

"There'll be other jobs. You know Nelly's friends are probably all movers and shakers. If I'm going to rub elbows with them, they have to treat me as an equal. And I'll be right in there, ready to snap up all their legal work."

"Oh." I draw a deep breath. I'm sickened. "Um...when are you going to get it?"

"I agreed to bring my trade-in down and finish up the paperwork soon. Before Christmas. Jen and I'll cruise down. It'll be a nice boat ride and a great sea trial for the new boat."

"Oh."

"That's all you can say? Just, oh? How about *hey that's awesome honey, good for you honey, you deserve it, honey.*"

"Good for you," I mumble.

He must've caught the sarcasm in my tone because now he turns to me, cheerful smile gone. "I know you don't want me to have a nice boat, Carly. You and your whining about a car that you certainly don't need when you can take a cab whenever you need to. Which is too damn often. Duffy says his wife orders groceries online and then she just parks outside the store and they bring them out. I want you to start doing that."

"But I don't have a computer, so I can't order online."

"Right. So you tell me what you want, I'll place the order and pick it up. That will stop all the impulsive buying you've been doing that's running the grocery bill up. That last one was a doozie and I don't see much in the fridge to show for it."

"It was, er, you know, staples like rice and flour."

"Do you think we have to stock up for the next Covid-19 shelter-in-place order, dummy? If so, you can quit because that's over and done. This will save time and money. We'll start immediately. I'll call the cab company and cancel the account."

"But—"

"But nothing!" He starts to get up as if he's going to come toward me.

I shrink back, bumping against the wall. "No, that's a good idea. Really a good idea. And I'm so proud of you! I really am! I'm glad for you, too! You're finally getting the recognition you deserve!"

He stops and sits back down, mollified. The hockey report resumes and he's no longer interested in me. I release the breath I didn't know I was holding.

I'm glad? He's finally getting the recognition he deserves? I'm surprised I didn't choke on those lies. I feel those burnt cookies churning in my stomach. For a moment I study the back of his head. His perfect hair. His perfect profile. His delicate hands. It's funny, but just last summer I had myself convinced I was lucky this beautiful man was my husband. Today Lita's words come back to me. *Derek is a chump.* She's right. I didn't see it before, but I do now. I experience an unfamiliar feeling: loathing.

He glances my way and frowns when he realizes I'm still standing here and that I've been studying him. I can almost hear him saying *what are you looking at? Haven't you got something to do?* Before he has a chance to say anything, I turn and escape back to the kitchen.

He's a chump, all right, and I've been a chump for believing him.

I can't wait to get on the internet.

Twenty-one

Lita

By a happy accident, I found the most excellent store to shop for a gift for Nullah. There was a road closure due to a watermain break and the detour went right past The Harbour Chandler. It doesn't look like much from outside, but the name was intriguing enough that I found a parking spot half a block away and walked back to check it out. Inside, there's everything you could ever need for your boat. And it turns out, the guy who helped me knows Nullah and his boat. He knew of something he needed and gave me a deal. I came home with a wireless handset for his radio. I'm pretty stoked about it.

I've finished wrapping it, congratulating myself when I compare it to Nullah's professionally-wrapped gift and conclude it measures up well. I've just put it up on the mantel when the truck belonging to the man in question drives into the yard. I scurry into the kitchen, get a glass of wine, and I'm on the loveseat in the family room sipping it and peeling off my nylon knee-highs when he comes in.

"Hello," I call out, "I'm in here!"

"Hello, babe," he calls back.

I hear him fussing around in the mudroom, probably taking off his shoes and hanging up his jacket. Then I hear the fridge door open and close and the snap of a beer can opening. He comes into the family room and bends down to give me a quick kiss before taking his customary place in the recliner in the corner.

"How was your day?" he asks.

"Fine. Good, actually," I respond. "Yours?"

"Okay."

"Just okay? Problems?"

"Not really problems. A machine in the thirty-minute workout circuit packed it in. The usual complaints about the usual offenders not disinfecting machines after using them. One lady wanted to speak to me about it. And I had to notify a couple of customers the delivery of their machines would be a week or so later than I originally said. They knew they wouldn't get them until after Christmas anyway, so they were okay with it."

"So...?"

"A couple of things about Derek," he says. He takes a long swallow of beer before continuing. "Did I tell you Finn hired a P.I. to vet him?"

"Um, I guess I knew you were vetting him. Didn't know what it involved, though."

"Well, call us paranoid. We do a pretty in-depth background check."

"So? I thought you called it off."

"We did. But the P.I. sent the info he already had on file before we called him off. Did you know he lived in Phoenix before he came here?"

"Sure."

"Do you remember the name Wayne Wilton?"

"Hmm. Sounds familiar, I guess because it's Derek's last name."

"Well, it was a minor news story about twenty years ago, boating accident. His wife drowned."

"Oh. And he's related to Derek?"

"He *is* Derek. He just started using his middle name when he came to Canada."

"Oh my god!" I gasp. "He's sure about this?"

"He's sure."

"We knew his first wife drowned. We just thought, oh poor guy, losing his wife like that."

"Yeah, well, I don't think you have to feel too sorry for him," Nullah says. "They thought it was suspicious."

"You mean maybe it wasn't an accident?"

"Right. The cops called it a Scott Peterson copycat murder. They could never find enough to charge him with it but the file still isn't closed, and they still call him a person of interest."

"Oh my god!" I exclaim. Is Derek really capable of deliberately drowning someone? It doesn't seem possible. But then, I wouldn't have thought anyone capable of drowning puppies or kittens, and thousands of people can do that."

"Yeah. Sweet guy. We're well rid of him. Except we're not really rid of him. Which brings me to the second thing," Nullah continues. "You won't believe it, but he seems to think I'm his new best friend. He invited me to a Christmas meet and greet his firm is having on Friday. He wants me to bring some friends."

"Really? That's, er..."

"Odd? Out of the blue? Gotta give him credit, he's got balls. Of course, he doesn't know that I know about him making that drug-dealing allegation. But I'll tell you what. He's pissing off the wrong people."

"What do you mean? You?"

"Well, I'm pissed, as you know, but I've got nothing to hide." He swigs his beer and looks off into the distance with a frown for a second, then says, "I can't say the same for some of my friends."

"Does he think you'll bring all your drug-dealing friends so he can pass along their names?"

"That's a possibility."

"*What?* You actually have drug-dealing friends?"

"I told you some of my friends aren't squeaky clean."

"I thought you meant shady business dealings or...oh, I don't know what I thought."

"Anyway. Maybe he thinks my friends are captains of industry and his partners will be impressed. Plus, it would give him a chance to brag.

In hopes he can snag their legal business. Either way, a win for him, I guess."

"Well, a lot of your friends *are* business owners."

"Yeah, well. You know, there are a couple who run businesses he might rather not be connected to."

"You're not thinking of going, are you?"

"I said I have a conflict. But then on the drive home, I thought, what if I took Alf. Get Alf to bring some of his buddies, and that they should wear their cuts."

"Speaking of businesses Derek might not want to be connected to."

"Exactly."

"Well, I imagine bikers have need of lawyers as much as anyone."

"Maybe more so, but does Derek's firm do criminal law?"

"Dunno," I admit. "Check their website."

"Naw, I don't really care." He takes a long swallow of beer. "Wouldn't I love to see Derek bragging himself up to those guys."

"Maybe he'd be smart enough to just keep his piehole the fuck shut for a change."

"I would like to see that, too. But mostly I'd love to embarrass the fucker in front of his partners."

"Would they go? Alf, I mean?"

"Maybe. Like I said, I got nothing to hide but looking at me turned up some, er, *links* I have with them. Cops have been leaning on them more than usual. They don't think it's a coincidence. Like I said, Wilton's pissing off the wrong people, so they might like to scare him a little. Shake him up. Plus, the boys wouldn't mind the free booze. Imagine what Derek's bosses, not to mention the other guests, would think if a dozen choppers roared up, parked in front of the building and the guys in their colors came in to mingle with guys in designer suits and Italian loafers."

"Do it! And take lots of video."

"Naww. I don't think so. I would if I thought the price of his guests' booze would come out of his own pocket, though." He picks up the remote, turns on the TV and starts flipping through the guide before settling on Global National. "What're you doing, sitting here in the dark staring at the blank TV screen, anyway?"

"I, er, just got here."

"Oh yeah?"

"Yeah. I was just enjoying a few minutes of the house being quiet before all hell breaks loose as it always does the minute you get home."

He runs the volume up to ear splitting and raises his voice to be heard above it. "TV being on is all hell breaking loose in your opinion?"

Then he laughs like it's the funniest thing he's ever said, turns the volume back down. "You should've seen your face."

"Very funny."

"I see you finally got me a gift." He indicates the mantel with a lift of his chin.

"Don't get too excited. It's just a chunk of coal."

"It's the thought that counts."

When the next commercial comes on, he mutes the TV, turns to me and says, "You know, the more I think about it, the more I like the idea of inviting Alf and his buddies. They don't like wife beaters any more than they like someone bringing heat down on them. Maybe Alf could find an opportunity to take the shithead aside and just quietly let him know some of the things he's been doing and saying might be hazardous to his health. Suggest that he should think twice before he flaps his gums about things that are none of his business, and while he's at it, quit calling me."

"I'm pretty sure you can get that last bit across to him yourself," I say. Then I realize the only way he could have Nullah's number is if Nullah gave it to him. "Surely to god you didn't give him your number."

"Of course not. He calls the gym. He drove the staff crazy leaving messages."

I shake my head. "I'm sorry that hooking up with me has visited this pestilence upon you."

"So far it's been worth it." He manages to make a leer look cute. "I hope this is the only pestilence in your history though, or you're going to have to up your game."

I ball up my knee highs and throw them at him. It's a perfect lob; he catches the incoming missile in his peripheral vision and brings up his arm to ward it off, but not in time. The socks bounce off his nose.

"Hey!"

"I'm going to have to up my game?" I ask. "How's that for game? A perfect Nullah bull's eye."

With astonishing speed, he puts his beer down, leaps to his feet and is on me. He picks me up, throws me across his shoulder in a fireman's carry, trots up the few steps to the bedroom level and into the master suite. He dumps me on the bed and climbs on top of me. "And there we have a perfect Lita Try. Five points for Nullah!" He unzips my pants and starts working them, along with my panties, down as he says, "And now a conversion for the extra two points."

I laugh and want to say, I didn't know a try was worth five points and also a bull's eye counts fifty, so he needs ten more tries to win on points. I should also offer to hit him in the nose with smelly socks more often since it's such a turn on. But feeling his body hard against mine, with those hands going places, somehow I'm okay with letting him think he's the winner. This time, anyway.

Twenty-two

Carly

Monday morning. I can hardly wait for Derek and Jennifer to leave. I'm distracted, mentally running over the inventory of his desk file drawer, wondering which file he would have the WIFI information in, or alternately, what a router looks like. I'm so excited I'm jittery. So jittery, my hands are shaking and when I top up his coffee, Derek notices.

"What's wrong with you?" he demands.

"Nothing."

"Nothing? Why are your hands shaking?"

"I, er, I'm just thinking about this new, um, there's this new recipe I'm going to try."

He rolls his eyes, but my reason is feeble enough to satisfy him. He frowns and shakes his head. Brainless Carly, all giddy at the thought of trying a new recipe. It's a lie he accepts without question.

I'm tempted to head for Derek's study as soon as I see the tail lights going out onto the road, but force myself to have a second cup of coffee and watch the news. I have this niggling fear he might have forgotten something, or noticed he had navy socks instead of black, or had some other reason to come back. It's never happened, but Murphy's Law, this would be the one time it did.

What would he do if he did have navy socks instead of black because I screwed up his sock drawer again, and came home to find me in his study? I indulge in the meat-tenderizer-hammer-to-the-head fan-

161

tasy. Then I think about all the hammers out in the garage. Would a bigger, heavier one be better? Should I go and get one? Hide it somewhere?

I tell myself not to be ridiculous. I would never actually do it. But just thinking that I'm not completely defenceless is empowering, whether I'd actually be able to follow through or not. The meat tenderizer hammer is pretty heavy, but it's not very big and something with a longer handle would be better. I'll do it. I think it will fit perfectly between the microwave and the wall and if he notices, I can say I used it to tap in those nails on the front deck rail that were popping on front deck rail. I stuck it behind the microwave to get it out of the way and forgot about it. Out of sight, out of mind. He'd be annoyed, but not enough to do anything. I'm going to do it.

Planning something like that. Having a fantasy like that. I must be truly evil.

Twenty-three

Lita

It's the first Friday night I've spent home alone since I moved in with Nullah and I miss him. Soon this will be more commonplace, and I will go out without him, too. This is normal. We're in a committed relationship; I wouldn't cheat on Nullah and I believe he is as trustworthy as I am.

Having these thoughts surprise me. I never thought I was the jealous type, but when I think about what gorgeous, successful women will be at the meet and greet, I have a moment of self doubt. I tell myself it's not Nullah I'm worried about, its those women. I don't trust them not to hit on him. He's so good looking I can't blame them, because I did it. That's how we got together after all. But neither of us was in a relationship so that was different. I tell myself it wouldn't matter how they came on to him, the worst he might do would be to flirt back and then come home horny. I call women like that missionaries. Before Nullah, I was one myself.

At last there are headlights coming up the drive, and minutes later, Nullah comes through the back door, calling out, "I'm home!"

"Hey! I'm in here," I respond. I stand and go to greet him with a kiss. He pulls me in tight and makes it a truly juicy one. So, I guess there was some missionary work going on. Just as I thought.

"Mmmm," I murmur, palm the growing bulge in his jeans, and say, "I guess you missed me."

"I miss you whenever we're apart, babe. But how come you're still up?"

"Just waiting for you," I tell him. "You reek of booze and cigarette smoke. I can't believe they allow smoking in that office."

"They don't. That was after."

"After what?"

"After the fancy schmancy meet and greet. I'm bushed. You ready for bed?"

"Um hmm," I agree, and follow him to the bedroom. I take my robe off, hang it on the back of the door, and slide between the sheets, half sitting as I watch him strip. "So! Don't keep me waiting. What about after? What about Derek?"

He disappears into the closet and comes back out naked, his penis at half mast. He climbs into bed, pulling me into his arms, and as I snuggle into his armpit he says, "That's better."

"Did Alf and his crew show up?"

"Did they ever! Nine of them. *Mmmmmmn*," he mumbles as he runs his hand down my ribs, then cups my buttock.

"So...?"

"So, they pretty well cleaned up everything on the food table, and made a good start on the booze. The bartender seemed to be enjoying himself and poured doubles without being asked. The good-looking young guy—"

"Ray?"

"Yeah. You met him once and you remember his name? You remember the other guys' names?"

"Umm, sure. I'm good with names."

"Okay, name them."

"There's, er, Bill. And Dave..."

"Forget it. There's no Bill or Dave. Figures you'd remember the young good-looking one. Anyway, Ray caught the eye of one of the caterers and they disappeared for a while."

"Oh yeah? Well, goodnight then. That's all I waited up to hear."

He chuckles. "I made sure to introduce everyone to the big boss, Jackson, and assured him we were all friends of Derek's and it was good of him to invite everyone. He was polite, but the way he was looking at Derek! I think Derek's gonna have some 'splainin' to do!" He growls deep in his throat and tries to pull me up on top of him.

I push him away. "Continue."

He snorts, but says, "Wilton was real friendly with one of the women. Good lookin' brunette. She seemed pretty happy with his attention. You'd think he'd be careful about it, but it was almost like he was showing off, like he wanted me to think he's a player. Had his arm around her and his hand practically on her tit when he introduced her to me. When the two of them went out into the hall like they were on the way to the washrooms, Alf was right behind and didn't let him follow her into the ladies room. Herded him down the hall and around the corner before, er, talking to him. Alf came back without him. The boys all grabbed bottles from behind the bar and left. I hung around until the slimy little fucker came back. He looked like he'd been crying. Jackson buttonholed him the second he came in and then he took off without saying anything to anyone else. Alf told me later that he grabbed him by the nuts to deliver the message. He thinks he may have squeezed a little harder than necessary and maybe there was a little twist, too. I guess I might feel like crying, too, if Alf got my junk in one of his meat hooks. You've seen the mitts on that guy."

"Oh! But you left early, then?"

"Yeah, booze and food cleaned up, message delivered. No reason to hang around. We went to the clubhouse and played poker. The caterer girl came away with Ray. Pretty sure she doesn't have a job anymore."

"You went to the clubhouse instead of coming home?"

"They did me a favor, babe. I couldn't just say see ya later. I lost enough that it wasn't rude for me to leave but I still got razzed for leaving early. They think I'm pussy-whipped. Afraid of a girl half my size. I told 'em you've got some nasty moves that make up for your size."

"Great. There goes any chance I have of getting with Ray."

"Want to get with an outlaw biker, do ya? You'll have to settle for an outlaw fitness club owner." He grasps my hips and pulls me up on top of him. "No more talk, babe. Show me some of those nasty moves, and make it quick. I'm tired."

"You're obviously ready, but I'm not. You're going to have to put a little more effort into it, buster."

He rolls on top of me. "*Arrgh*! They're right. I *am* pussy whipped."

He starts to work his way down, fondling and kissing everything on his way while he mutters about me not knowing who's boss and promises that what he's about to do will have me begging for mercy, just before his head disappears under the covers.

Does he really think he's the boss? I'm going to have a discussion with him about that. Some other time.

Twenty-four

Carly

I'm in bed, tossing and turning, unable to fall asleep. This isn't unusual. It makes Derek crazy because when I'm thrashing around he can't fall asleep either. Not that he's here now. I was hoping to be sound asleep before he got home from the company party.

On nights like this I often take my pillow and go downstairs to sleep in the recliner. It's uncomfortable, though, and I can't sleep very long that way. I wish Derek would agree to get a bed for the spare room. But as he points out, we never have overnight guests so it would be a waste of money. I decide that if I'm still awake at one, I'll go down to the recliner. But then I hear the car drive in, and glance at the clock. 11:18. That's kind of early. I hope nothing went wrong.

The car door slams then the back door opens and closes. There's a crashing noise and the sound of glass breaking. Did he knock the vase off the console table in the foyer? He must be drunk, probably shouldn't have driven home, and will no doubt want sex. It'll be mercifully short, but still, it's a rough, thoroughly unpleasant experience when he's drunk, but I learned early on not to refuse. Too late now to escape to the recliner. I'll have to pretend to be asleep.

He pushes the bedroom door open with such force it slams back against the wall, and flicks the switch to turn on the ceiling lights. No way anyone could possibly sleep through that.

"You're home," I mumble. I roll onto my back, fake a yawn and stretch. "How was the party?"

He pulls his jacket and tie off and throws them on the chair. "Oh, it was awesome, honey. Just *fuckin'* awesome."

"Oh. Good." I roll to my side so my back is to him and burrow into my pillow, hoping that's the end of the conversation.

"Yeah, Nelly really made an impresshun with the big guys. Showed up with a bunch of his frienz. Fuckin' pigs ate all the food... like a swarm of filthy fuckin' locuss."

Pigs? Locusts? Oh, no. I shrink further under the covers.

"And drink? Half the time they never fuckin' waited to be served. Just fuckin' helped themselves. When they left, they took booze with them. Nearly fuckin' cleaned us out."

What kind of friends does Nullah have, anyway? I'm not going to ask. Derek swearing like that means he's really angry and that doesn't bode well for me. I say nothing in hopes he gets into bed and passes out.

But he comes to my side of the bed and I hear him breathing heavily. Then he grabs me by the hair and hauls me off the bed. I land heavily, my feet tangled in the sheets.

"Get up!" he hisses.

I struggle to untangle myself and sit up.

"I said, *get the fuck up!*"

"I am! I am!" I sob, manage to disentangle myself and stand. He grabs the front of my pyjamas and propels me back against the wall. I brace for the first blow.

But it doesn't come.

"You fuckin' bitch! What did you tell your little friend? Fuckin' Lita?" His face is inches from mine. He's spraying saliva with every word and his heavy alcohol breath nearly gags me. "'Course you'd never tell her you have it comin', would you? You wouldn't tell her anything to make me look bad, you said. You think talking about our private lives, our fuckin' marriage, that helps me? You think Nelly likes me more now?"

"Oh, but I... I didn't!"

"Of course you fuckin' did! How'd anyone know... How'd Nelly find out if you didn't?"

"I—"

"Don't!"

He releases me and takes a couple of steps away, bumping against the bed and abruptly sitting on it. I start away, but he gets unsteadily to his feet and grabs the back of my pyjama tops. "You wanna leave? Good! Go! Fuckin' get outta here before I change my mind." He shoves me. I stumble forward, putting my hands up at the last second to avoid going face first into the wall. "F'now on, you don't sleep in my bed until I sums...summon you."

I turn to face him. He's coming toward me, his face twisted with rage. I dash for the door and make it out into the hallway. I don't want him to catch me on the stairs, so I hurry down. When I look back up, I realize he's not behind me. The bedroom door slams shut.

I have no idea why the attack stopped. I'm relieved but at the same time, puzzled. I can't believe it, but Lita must have told Nullah that Derek abused me, even though I begged her not to tell anyone. Worse, she told Nullah, and he must've said something to him at that party. This not only doesn't help Derek, but it makes things worse for me. He'll never let me near anyone again.

I'm starting toward the kitchen when I experience an intense pain in my foot. Too late I remember the crashing sound. I turn on the lights in the foyer and examine my foot. It's bleeding, and there's glass from the broken vase on the floor. I pick up the largest pieces then choose my steps carefully as I make my way to the bathroom and put a Band-Aid on my foot. Then I get a broom and dustpan from the broom closet and sweep the entire area before going into the kitchen.

Derek still hasn't come back down. I wonder if he's going to stay up there. Is it safe to make a cup of camomile tea? It wouldn't be un-usual for him to come back after me once he's had a chance to think about what else I might have done that deserves punishment. But so far, I don't hear any movement upstairs.

Is the only punishment he can think of banning me from our bed? If he had done that last summer I would've been devastated but it's been months since I wanted to even be near him. Why? It's not like the abuse is something new. What happened to make me see him in a different way?

Lita. Lita happened.

HAVING SLEPT IN THE recliner in the family room, I'm the first one up in the morning. I get everything ready to make French toast, bacon, and maybe hash browns, in hopes that if Derek is still angry when he comes down, the nice breakfast will put him in a better mood. I remind myself Jennifer should be down soon. In fact, she has to be taken to the airport this morning, so I'm likely safe.

I don't expect Derek up before noon, long after Jennifer has to leave. I look forward to being the one to take her. It's been so long since I had the car. Maybe I can zip into Ladysmith before I come home. I don't really need anything, but it would be nice just to stroll along and look at the shops. Now that I'm able to get on the internet, I know the kitchen shop has a sale this weekend and even posted a coupon for an extra 10% off. I'd love to check it out, even though I have no money to buy anything.

I hear footfalls on the stairs and expect it to be Jennifer, but instead it's Derek, bleary-eyed and unkempt, his hairy legs sticking out under his crookedly-belted robe. Was it only a few months ago I would've focused on the little patch of silky hair that shows in the vee of his robe and thought myself lucky that this sexy man was my husband? And I would've been disappointed and thought it was a failure on my part that he didn't kiss me?

"Oh," I say, "I thought you'd sleep in this morning."

He says nothing, just goes into the fridge, gets a beer and pours it into a glass, then roots around in the pantry until he comes out with a can of Clamato juice. Once he tops up the beer with that, he mumbles, "Tabasco?"

I open the spice cabinet, find the bottle, and hand it to him.

He shakes several squirts into his glass, then asks, "What time does Jennifer have to be at the airport?"

"I, uhh, er, the kids are supposed to meet with the chaperones at 10:30. But you don't have to go. I can take her."

"I'll take her," he says. He gets a cup of coffee and takes it, his red eye and his iPad into the family room.

I was looking forward to taking her but I know there's no use arguing. I follow him to the family room, stopping at the top of the stairs, and ask, "I'm making French toast. Would you like bacon and hash browns with that?"

"Forget the fuckin French toast. Just make me plenty of bacon and hash browns, and a couple eggs." Then he looks up at me through narrowed eyes and adds, "And Carly? I'm golfing this afternoon, so I won't be home until dinner time. But don't think we're finished talking about last night. You know how you're always bragging about being the star of the Rip Tides? We'll take a little boat ride and find out if you can still swim as well as you did in swim club."

My guts clench. I know what that means. He has threatened to toss me overboard before but he wouldn't really do it. Not when he's had all day to calm down.

Still. Usually by morning, he's over whatever upset him. But he doesn't seem angry. He's calm. Maybe a nice big dinner complete with made-from-scratch Hollandaise sauce and dessert will appease him. Cook your man happy, my mother always said.

I wonder why I'm just now realizing that it didn't work for her.

Twenty-five

Lita

The wind is increasing and the not-too-bad-just-a-little-rough chop turned to surge waves half an hour ago. This fishing trip/boat ride is becoming a truly miserable experience. For the past forty-five minutes give or take, the radio has been squawking with reports from other boaters describing the same situation where they are, which is pretty much up and down the coast. Nullah is constantly checking the screen on the Chart Plotter for the weather report, which only confirms what we know firsthand: there's a storm going on.

My stomach starts to churn and I wonder if there's a bucket somewhere that I could have near me in case I can't make it to the head. I'm reminded of the line from that silly song, something about my head is hung over the rail and I fear I will dirty the ocean. *Hasten, Jason, bring the basin! Oops, stop, bring the mop.*

Nullah glances my way. "Sorry, babe," he says, "this is getting pretty rough. Looks like that southeaster that wasn't supposed to hit until later tonight is blowin' in ahead of schedule."

"I knew we should've stayed in bed."

"You were right." He fusses with the radio, listens to a few more reports, then asks, "I guess you're out of Gravol?"

The expression on my face must be telling, because he doesn't wait for my response.

"You know," he says, "I think instead of heading back to Nanaimo, we should put in to Silva Bay. We can tie up and wait out the storm there."

"But what if it doesn't let up by dinner time? All we've got is chips."

"I can't believe you're actually thinking about eating."

"I was thinking of you."

"Aww, that's nice, you're thinking about eating me. But that's for later. For dinner, we have a fish, remember?" He doesn't exactly chuckle but he's definitely highly amused. "Don't think the pub's open but there's a convenience store next to the marina office. They might have Gravol but if not, we can at least grab some Ding Dongs. So there's fish, chips, and dessert."

Ding Dongs? Fish? Is he trying to make me puke? He's never had a seasick day on the water so maybe it's impossible for him to empathize, but does he have to actually enjoy my misery? I doubt my glare is convincing but lacking something at hand to throw at him, that's the best I can do. I clamp my jaw shut and swallow furiously to stem my rising gorge.

"I'm sorry, babe," Nullah says, "I wish we'd stayed home, too. But Silva Bay is close, and it's sheltered. Even if the pub and restaurant aren't open, at least we can go ashore. A walk on solid land should settle your seasickness. We could head back to Nanaimo, but it would mean another hour of rough seas and judging by how green you look, I think you'd be a whole bunch happier in Silva Bay even if we end up having to overnight there."

I note the tension in his shoulders and his hands white-knuckled on the helm. The sea is so high we're being tossed around like a cork. Nullah heads the boat into a roller that nearly lifts me off my chair. He handles the boat well and would say it was unsafe to try and get home if there was any danger, but even though the boat is perfectly capable of navigating in a storm like this and it might be better once we got to Northumberland Channel, what's the point? Tying up at the nearest sheltered moorage until it blows over is the sensible choice. At least that's what my stomach thinks.

"Silva Bay, here we come."

Twenty-six

Carly

H is car turns into the driveway and my guts clench. I've been ob-
sessing about this all day. Has he forgotten this morning's
threat? If not, I tell myself we might continue the so-called conversation, as one-sided as our conversations always are, but the worst he
would do would be the usual. A broken nose or wrist is survivable,
while being in the cold water for more than a few minutes would be a
death sentence. He wouldn't really haul me down to the boat and throw
me overboard. He's rough and he has a temper, but he's not a murderer.

But what if this time, he does mean it? At what point will I know
for sure? If he tries anything, I'll fight back. I have the hammer. I have
to decide where the cut-off is. Do I wait until he punches me? What
if he punches me so hard I can't fight back, and then takes me down
to the boat? At what point do I get the hammer and use it on him? It
would have to be sudden. I can't just threaten him with it because he'd
be able to overpower me and take it away. Maybe use it on me! If it can't
be sudden... If I can't get to it... If I can't actually use it on his head... I'll
refuse to move so he'll have to carry me.

Then I think about how strong he is and how weak I am by compar-
ison. I'm fat, but he outweighs me by twenty pounds. I guess it's true,
muscle weighs more than fat. I think of the times he's hauled me out on
the front deck and easily hoisted me up on the rail and no amount of
struggling, planting my feet, or flailing my arms did any good. He holds
me so that if he were to let go, I'd fall, and it's a drop of at least three

yards. When he lifts me down off the rail, he always laughs and says, *you shouldn't sit up there like that. It's not safe.*

What if he lets go this time? I could survive the fall but even if I didn't break anything, he could come and catch me. He wouldn't have to carry me; he could just drag me the rest of the way. It's rough but it's downhill, so even I could drag a body down. I imagine being dragged feet first down the trail, my head bouncing off rocks, trying to save myself by grabbing bushes. Trying to protect my head. I clench my teeth and force the image out of my head.

Except for the finishing touches, dinner is ready. If he's still mad, maybe it will be enough.

He comes in through the back door. In a moment, he appears in the kitchen. I can't quite read his expression, so I say, "Hi, honey. How was your day? Did the band's flight get away okay? How was your golf round?"

He doesn't answer but surprises me by coming to give me a kiss. Then he asks, "What's for dinner?"

"Umm, well, schnitzel with mushrooms and home-made spaetzle. Cherries jubilee for dessert. All your favorites." I risk a smile.

He doesn't smile back but looks happy in a weird sort of way. Relief floods through me. There's a stain on his shirt as if he spilled something on it. He must've gone into the clubhouse after golf and had just enough drinks to mellow him out. He says, "Great. Is it ready?"

"Yes. Or it will be in ten minutes."

"Perfect." He leaves and I hear his keys rattling. He's making the rounds, locking up the house for the night. When he comes back, he gets a beer out of the fridge and takes it to his usual seat at the kitchen table, apparently to watch me while he waits.

I heat the frying pan, put the schnitzels in it to warm through, and microwave the gravy with its load of sliced mushrooms. When the gravy's out, I put the steamed broccoli spears in and warm them. Butter is melting in another pan and I toss the cooked spaetzle in that. In under ten minutes, dinner is plated and I bring both dishes to the table. As I slide Derek's in front of him, he says, "Don't bother sitting down, Carly."

"You need something?"

"No, but you shouldn't eat dinner. You know it's not wise to eat before you swim." He looks up at me and I realize the expression of a few minutes ago that I thought was weird but happy, is just weird. His eyes. His hideous grin. He's the picture of a madman. "You don't want to get a cramp."

He's not kidding. I draw a quick breath. "But Derek—"

He slams his fist on the table, making the plates and cutlery rattle. "No *but Derek*! You're always bragging about all the prizes you won when you were in swim club. Here's your chance to show off. And you've got plenty of blubber to keep you warm."

I'm stunned and can't move.

He shovels spaetzle and gravy into his mouth, then snorts and says, "Don't worry. I'm not crazy. It's a miserable, stormy night. I won't take you more than a few hundred yards out. It's just payback for blabbing to your little friend. And it doesn't leave a mark, so you'll have nothing to show her. Not that you'll ever see her again." He seems calm and reasonable as he turns his attention on his dinner.

I'm still standing, plate in hand, unable to think. Then I realize he means what he's saying. He's enjoying it, toying with me like a cat tormenting a mouse. I think about smashing my plate on his head and running, but I'd never get out the door before he caught me. In a flash of insight, I realize why he locked the deadbolts when he did, and why he had insisted on deadbolts with no thumb turns in the first place. Not to stop thieves from carrying big stuff out as he claimed at the time, but to lock someone in. Me. He's been planning this for years. There's no way out.

When he looks at me again, it's with a dark frown and he asks, "What're you looking at?"

I retreat to the other side of the peninsula and put my plate on the counter. My heart is racing and I break out in a sweat. I'm breathing so quickly I'm nearly panting. I need to call for help.

I go to the foyer, to the console table where I always keep my phone. It's not there. I move the centerpiece. Nothing. Did I leave it in my purse? It's hanging on the hallstand. I frantically root through it, checking both compartments twice. It's not there, and there's nowhere else I would have put it.

I hear Derek snigger and turn to see him standing in the short hall leading to the kitchen. "Looking for this?" he asks, and pulls my phone out of his pants pocket. My heart sinks.

I whirl, grab the newel post, and race up the stairs, taking two at a time. I hear him laughing as he follows me, slowly, knowing that short of jumping from a window, there's no escape. All he has to do is wait for me to come out.

But then, he wants to go and get the new boat in the morning, so he won't want to wait long. I dart into the bathroom, lock the door, and lean back against it.

"Carly!" he sings my name. "Carly, baby! Come on out, Carly!"

"Go away!" I yell, knowing it will do no good.

"Come on out, Carly! I want to finish my dinner, and then I'll be wanting dessert."

He calls my name over and over, then all is quiet. I wonder if he's gone back downstairs. It doesn't matter, because it won't be safe for me to go out again until tomorrow, when he's on his way down to Sidney in his boat. I have a stab of increased fear when I think he might postpone that trip. Then I'll have to wait in here until he goes to work on Monday. 6:37. I'll be imprisoned for a long time either way.

Suddenly, something hits the door with a crash, and I can't help screaming. Does he think he can break the door down? *Can* he break it down?

Then it sounds like a full body slam against the door. Again. The door springs open and he's standing there smiling, his fists opening and closing. I back away until I bump up against the vanity. My hand closes around something. A candle in a glass jar. I throw it at him. He ducks. The candle sails past him and bounces along the carpet in the hall.

With a lunge, he's on me and has me by the hair. I pummel him with my fists but all that does is make him laugh. I realize not putting that hammer in my pocket was a deadly mistake. But then, I have no pockets. I always imagined I'd be in the kitchen and would be able to grab it.

He pulls me away from the wall, lets go of my hair long enough to grab my arm and twist it up behind me, then pushes me to the door and out into the hall. I stumble, painfully wrenching my arm, but he keeps propelling me toward the stairs. Will he push me down them? I manage to grasp the handrail with my free hand. He slows a bit. So, he doesn't want me to fall? A small mercy.

When we get to the kitchen, I see his plate is still on the table, but he's finished eating the food. So that's what he was doing when it went quiet. He releases my arm and gives me a shove.

I retreat to the far side of the peninsula. My heart is racing. I try to calm myself so I can think rationally by slowing my breathing, holding my breath for a count of seven, breathing out and not inhaling again for a count of seven.

The little steel meat tenderizer hammer is in the sink. The big hammer is beside the microwave. Can I sneak up on him? He'd never let me get behind him and if I came at him face to face and took a swing with the hammer, he'd grab it and take it away from me. I'll have to wait for an opportunity to get behind him.

He stands blocking me so I can't leave the work area of the kitchen, watching me.

"Derek, please! I didn't tell Lita anything, not really. Just girl talk. She asked if you ever hurt me, because you slapped her that time—"

"The lying, fucking cunt! I never slapped her."

"Oh, er, I... You mean, that was a lie?"

"What do you think?"

I can't tell him what I really think. Given what he's done to me, why wouldn't I believe her? But I focus on keeping my voice low and calm. "You know, I didn't believe her. But she cornered me into telling her about that time after Finn... You know. Because she noticed the scar on my cheek. But I told her it was just that one time, and I deserved it. You didn't mean to cut me, it was just, um, your ring. I told her to forget it."

"Well, she didn't forget it. She told Nelly. You know those suspicions I had about him? I was right. There's more to him than you or Lita know about. He's in bed with some real shady characters. I'll be lucky if I keep my job after that fiasco last night. Jackson wants me in his office first thing Monday. Do you think I have enough savings to pay for all this," he waves his hand in a circle, "until I get another job? Thanks so much, you fat, ugly, stupid bitch!"

"I'm sorry, Derek! I'll talk to Lita. Tell her I made it all up. I'll say I made it all up because I was mad at you after we had an argument. Which, er, was my fault entirely—"

"That ship has sailed, honey. Time for me to cut my losses. One less big, fat mouth to feed. Now get busy."

"What do you mean?"

"Dessert. I want my dessert."

How can he be so calm? Is thinking about murdering me enjoyable? Is talking about it, telling me what he's going to do, part of the fun?

I wonder about the woman in the video on his laptop. Did she end up dead? I've heard of those things—snuff movies—but I never thought there could really be such a thing. Now I'm not so sure.

Visions of being dragged feet first down the trail to the beach flood my head. I swallow hard and concentrate on calming my beathing while my heart pounds. "Dessert?"

"You said you were making Cherries Jubilee." He goes to take his place at the table and adds, "I'll have a coffee, too. Make it a decaf. And Carly? Don't make me chase you again. It won't go so well a second time."

A strange calm settles over me.

I exhale loudly. "Decaf it is."

I put in a pod of decaf in the Keurig, and with a mug under the spout, hit the on button. While the coffee is brewing, I get the ice cream out of the freezer and put a scoop in one of the fancy cut-glass dessert dishes my grandmother gave me. I readied the cherries and made the two separate batches of sauce earlier; I select the one I need. Now all I have to do is warm everything up. I carefully pour Kirschwasser around the the mound of ice cream, cherries and sauce. When the coffee's done, I bring the mug and the Cherries Jubilee to the table and set them in front of Derek.

"Just don't light yourself on fire again," he says. He picks up his mug and takes a careful sip. "I'm surprised you're taking this so well. I guess you know you deserve punishment."

I manage to nod as I reach the lighter from the counter. "Yes. You're right. I should never have said anything to Lita. That was wrong of me."

He looks up at me and grins; I'm outwardly calm but my hands are so unsteady it takes three tries before the lighter produces a flame. I tip the dessert slightly so the flame licks the Kirschwasser and ignites it. In seconds, the alcohol burns off and the flames die. Derek picks up his spoon and scoops up sauce-covered ice cream.

Suddenly I change my mind. If I go through with this, my life is over. "No, Derek, wait!" I reach to take the dessert away.

He stabs my hand with the spoon, pinning it to the table.

"*Ahhh uhhh!*" I cry, and struggle to get my hand out from under the spoon.

He presses down harder and says, "Now look at this mess." Ice cream and sauce runs off the spoon and over my hand.

"Stop please, Derek! It really hurts!"

He pulls the spoon away and digs into his dessert as if nothing happened. I take a step back so I'm standing against the peninsula, massaging my hand while watching him devour the dessert. When he's finished, he looks up, pushes the dish toward me and says, "Why're you still standing there? Clean up the mess in the kitchen and then we're taking a walk down to the boat."

I don't move. A look of puzzlement comes over him, then it changes to concern. He sits bolt upright and tries to get up but collapses back into the chair.

It's happening. A sense of unreality washes over me. It's as if I've slipped into a murky quagmire where everything happens in slow motion. I go to sit next to him so we're eye to eye.

"Not feeling well?" I ask.

"Call an ambulance, Carly! I think I'm having a heart attack."

"It might feel like that," I tell him. "I ground up the cherry pits and put them in the sauce. From what I've read on the internet, ten should be enough to kill you. To be sure, I doubled that."

"The internet? How...?"

"Yeah, I've been on the internet. Don't like that, do you? I'm not the complete moron you thought I was."

"Carly," he wails, "help me!"

"Sorry, can't. No one can. But just so you know, this doesn't leave marks, either. It'll just look like a heart attack."

"Carly!" He gasps. His face becomes flushed as he struggles for breath. Seconds later, his body goes limp and he exhales. The stench of urine wafts up around me and I realize he's urinated, and all I feel is disgust. It's almost as if I'm watching from a distance. Like this is a snuff movie. I didn't know it would be so easy to murder him.

I give myself a mental shake, get up and go to the fridge for a glass of wine. I bring it and my dinner to the table and sit next to him to eat. I'm astonished at my lack of emotion when my life as I know it is over.

But then I realize I'm not without emotion. What I feel isn't re-morse, though, it's pride. I actually did it. I beat him. I won. I'm free of him at last. I think my first call will be to Lita to thank her for opening my eyes and giving me the courage to push my shame aside and get out of my abusive marriage.

"To your health," I tell say, raising my glass in Derek's direction be-fore taking a long swallow. His health? It strikes me as such a funny thing to say when he's so obviously dead his lips are turning blue. I erupt into paroxysms of laughter.

Twenty-seven

Lita

The southeaster is still blowing around us. The boat is bobbing, straining against the mooring lines, and rain lashes the cabin windows, but Nullah was right, the Silva Bay marina is sheltered enough that although it's windy, it's not really miserable.

We walk around the little section of Gabriola Island close to Silva Bay for long enough to get cold and wet, but at least my stomach returns to normal. We thought we'd get a cabin for the night, but the rentals are closed for the season. Thankfully, the marina office had Gravol, the boat isn't rocking and rolling terribly, so we're on board and will stay tied up here for the duration of the storm. The Oldies but Goodies rock channel is pumping out Bruce Springsteen, who's assuring us that this gun is for hire. I'm at the table in the cabin with my Kindle in front of me, halfway into the latest Toby Neale thriller, glass of wine at hand and doing okay.

Nullah is sitting across from me. Actually not sitting, *lounging* back in the corner of the banquette with his feet sticking out into the aisle, doing whatever on his phone. He's on his second beer and has nearly polished off an entire family size bag of barbeque-flavored chips. He can have them all. I hate that flavor.

My phone rings. I pick it up and see it's Carly calling. "That's odd," I mumble, and answer, putting it on speaker for Nullah's benefit.

"Hey, Carly! What's up?"

"Oh, not much. Just finished dinner."

"Us too," I reply. Derek wants Carly to keep sucking up so he's told her she can call me, but only when he's there, which is why we have our private conversations during working hours. I need to know if the asshole is listening in, so I ask, "Um, is Derek there?"

"He's here, yeah. But he can't talk."

Nullah looks up from his phone.

"Oh?" I say.

"Yeah. Actually, when I said there was not much up, that's not really true. I have news. I wanted you to be the first to hear it."

"You have news?"

"Yeah. Derek's dead."

Nullah sits bolt upright. She has our full attention now.

"What?" I gasp. "How? Was there an accident?"

"No, there was no accident," she says. "I killed him."

I feel as though the wind has been knocked out of me. I can't speak.

Carly continues, "Yeah, he's still sitting here next to me. Don't worry, I'm going to call the cops as soon as I get off the phone with you. I just wanted you to know I never would've had the courage to do it if you hadn't been there for me."

I gasp again. I'm the cause of her committing murder? I manage to find my voice and cry, "Oh my god, Carly!"

"Yeah. It's one hundred per cent thanks to you. I thought, Lita would never put up with any man doing to her what Derek does to me. He only slapped Lita once and she dumped him. And then I realized, it's not so much what he's done to me, but what I've let him do to me. So I'm partly to blame. I am so ashamed of letting him do it, time and time again. But that's all over now. I guess I'm calling to thank you."

"Carly, it's Nullah," Nullah chimes in. "I'm here with Lita—"

"Oh, hi, Nullah!" Carly cuts him off. "Hey, I don't know what's going to happen from here, but I want you to know—no, I want both of you to know—I'm glad Lita has you. I'm glad you're together."

"Er, thanks, I'm glad Lita has me, too," he says. "Carly, you haven't called anyone else? The cops?"

"No, but I'm going to do that as soon as I get off the phone with you."

"No, Carly! Before you call anyone else, let's talk about this," Nullah continues. "Tell you what. Don't do anything right now, just sit tight. Me and Lita are coming right over."

"But I need to call the police."

"Sure, but not right now. There's no hurry. You can call them after we get there. Because they'll come right away and they can be pretty rough. You need a friend with you. For moral support."

"Umm..."

"I want to be there with you, Carly," I say. I don't know if I've fully recovered from the shock of her news, but at least my brain is starting to boot up. "Where's Jennifer? The police will take you in, and there will be forensics people all over your place. We can take Jennifer home with us."

"No, she's gone to Ottawa with the school band."

"Oh. Okay, that's good."

"Still," Nullah says, "it's a good idea to have Lita with you. You know, as your friend, but also as your lawyer. You need your lawyer with you when the police are questioning you."

"Oh yeah," Carly says, "I didn't think of that. Derek says she only does insurance stuff, though."

"That's right," I tell her, "we'll get you a crim... er, a better lawyer right away, but at least I can hold down the fort until we figure out who'd be best. Okay?" I can hear her breathing while she thinks about it. "Okay?" I ask again.

"Okay," she agrees.

"Good! Then just sit tight until we get there."

"We'll be a little while," Nullah tells her. He's on his feet and reaching for his jacket. "We're not home right now, we're on the boat, on the east side of Gabriola Island. I'm not sure how long it'll take for us to get there. But don't worry, we're coming. Definitely. You can stay on the phone with Lita while I cast off."

"It's okay," Carly says, "I think I'll go up and shower."

I look at Nullah and mouth: *shower?*

"I, um, don't you want to stay on the line, Carly?" I ask.

"No, I'm fine. I'd like to shower, though. I've been so stressed all day, my armpits are really stinky."

"Just don't do anything else, then, honey," I tell her. "We'll be there as soon as we can."

"I'll watch for you," she promises, and the line goes dead.

"Oh, my god, Nullah!" I wail as I slide out from beside the table, "do you think she has to shower because she's covered in blood?"

He shakes his head and shrugs, his face grim. Pulling his floater jacket on, he heads for the door. "I'll get the mooring lines, you pull up the bumpers, and we'll get going."

"How long will it take us to get back to Nanaimo, put the boat away, and drive to Carly's? A couple of hours, at least? I hope she can sit tight that long."

"Instead of going back to Nanaimo, we'll take the boat and tie up at their wharf."

"Is it okay, in this storm?"

"As easy as going back to Nanaimo. We'll head south, then cut west between Pylades and DeCourcy. That'll put us in Dodd Narrows close to their dock."

I get my jacket on, follow him out the door, and pull up the bumpers while he coils the ropes and tosses them up on the deck. He jumps off the wharf onto the boat and we both go back into the cabin. He climbs onto the captain's chair, turns on the running lights and starts the engines. We chug slowly away from the wharf, and haven't gone far before the boat starts rocking and rolling again. He studies the screen on the chart plotter, checks all the other electronics as well, and we listen to the weather report. No good news there.

"Hang on," Nullah says. "Hope you don't run out of Gravol."

"Where's that basin," I mutter. My stomach is already squeezing. I imagine Carly killing Derek. If she bloodied herself so badly in the process that she needed a shower, there must be blood everywhere. Pooling on the floor. Cast off on the walls and ceiling. The sight of blood, as in someone wounded and bleeding, doesn't bother me, but visualizing a bloody murder scene and possibly a chopped-up body coupled with the boat being tossed around in the heavy seas might be too much for even a whole package of Gravol. Although I have little faith it'll help, I dry swallow two tablets, climb onto the First Mate's chair, and grip the grab bar with both hands.

Nullah looks away from the chart plotter for a second to give me a quick grin. "Get your life jacket on, babe," he says. He returns his attention to the screen and then scans our surroundings.

And I thought being seasick was my biggest worry! I take a couple of gulping swallows, then ask, "Is it safe to go through the Narrows now? In the dark? In this storm?"

"We're in luck. The water's rough but the tide's right now, best time to go. We should be able to catch the last of the fair current, and I doubt there'll be any other traffic, which is a good thing. We have nav, plus there's beacons. Don't worry."

Great. He says don't worry when he's just told me to put on a life jacket as we head into a storm to go to the scene of a murder. What's there to worry about?

Twenty-eight

Carly

I'm standing in the darkened foyer looking out into the night. I've already dug the keys out of Derek's pants pocket and unlocked the deadbolt, so now I'm just waiting for Lita and Nullah to drive in. How long before I should call the police? I know Nullah said not to do anything until they got here, but I'm beginning to get antsy. Then I remind myself no one is going to show up unannounced at midnight, find me with my husband's dead body, and say, oh Carly, he's dead. Why haven't you called someone? I guess if they did, I'd say I have called someone, my friends. My only friends.

I've just concluded there would be no random visitors when I'm startled by a knock at the back door. I rush through the house and turn on the outside light, but there's no way I can see who's there. I call, "Who is it?"

"It's us," Lita answers.

"Oh!" I pull the door open. "I didn't see anyone drive in. I was watching out the front. How did you get here?"

"We came on the boat and tied up at your dock. Shitty coming up that trail in the dark," Lita says.

"Well, you're soaking wet. Get in out of the rain."

As she comes in, Lita pulls me into a hug. Nullah closes the door and hovers behind us. She says, "Oh my god, Carly! What happened?"

Suddenly a wave of emotion floods through me and I start crying.

189

"Come on," Nullah says gently, "let's go in." He loops an arm around Lita and me and herds us into the kitchen. Now they see Derek, slouching bonelessly but still upright in a chair at the table. Nullah sidles past Lita and me and goes to Derek, pressing his fingers against his throat.

"He's dead, Nullah," I sob as I pull away from Lita. "No need to check."

"But he looks... What happened?" Lita asks. "How...?"

I get a Kleenex from the dispenser on the counter to blow my nose before replying. "Somehow he found out I told you about him, er, his abuse. Something must've happened at the company party because he came home from that hopping mad. Tonight he said he was going to take me out in the boat and throw me overboard to see if I could make it back to shore."

Nullah comes and puts a hand on my shoulder. "It's my fault, Carly. That was my fault. Let's go in the other room." He gives me a nudge and all three of us go out into the foyer and through to the living room. Lita and I sit on the loveseat while Nullah takes the armchair.

After a moment, I realize what Nullah said. "How was it your fault, Nullah?" I ask.

"Well, uh," he says, and squirms uncomfortably, "I, uh, had a friend speak to him at that party. I thought it would make him quit, er..."

"Oh. He invited you? I guess it didn't go quite the way he expected, then. But don't blame yourself, Nullah," I tell him, "he's been talking about me going for a swim for a while now. This is the first time I thought he really meant it, though."

"So, umm, how did you...?" Lita asks.

"Kill him?" I finish her sentence for her. "I fed him his favorite dessert."

"Poison," Nullah guesses. When I nod, he asks, "What kind?"

"Cyanide," I respond.

"Where'd you get cyanide?" Lita wants to know.

"It's in lots of things, Lita," I tell her. "You'd be surprised. Apple seeds. Peach pits. Trace amounts of it in lots of everyday food. But I used cherry pits."

"He ate cherry pits? That wouldn't kill anyone. I've swallowed them."

"No, swallowing a few cherry pits won't hurt anyone. It's only when they're cracked open. The bad part is inside, which unless they're split open, just passes right through you. I ground them up and put them in the sauce." I smile and shrug. "Very fast acting. I barely had time to tell him what I'd done before he died. And now, I should call the police."

"Just a sec," Nullah says. "So. Cyanide. I don't think you need to call anyone."

Lita gives Nullah an odd look and says, "What do you mean?"

"They don't test for cyanide poisoning. Medical examiners, I mean. Medical examiners don't test for cyanide. It looks like a heart attack."

"No one's going to think Derek had a heart attack," Lita opines, "not as young and fit as he is. Was. So they'll run more tests and might find out what, er..."

"What if we toss him in the salt chuck?" Nullah asks. "That's what he planned to do to Carly. Sort of fitting if he was the one who drowned."

"Nice idea, baby, but he won't have water in his lungs so they won't call it drowning, either," Lita concludes. "Maybe if she says it was an accident."

"How could it be an accident?"

"If she put the cherries in the blender to make the sauce and there was a pit she didn't notice."

"One pit wouldn't do it," Carly says. "Ten is a lethal dose. I gave him twenty. Anyone would notice that many in the blender."

They both stare, their expressions unreadable. Astonished, I guess. Nullah pulls out his phone.

"Who are you calling?" Lita asks.

"Not calling. Googling cyanide poisoning."

"I read it's undetectable after a couple of days," I tell them. "But I can't wait two days to report that he died."

"No. But if he's in the water for a couple of days before he's found..." Nullah grows quiet as he reads further.

"No water in his lungs," Lita reiterates.

"What if he was taking a leak over the side when a wave rocked the boat and he fell in? The cold water could've been enough of a shock to stop his heart before he sucked in any water. And all the body's, er, processes, don't stop just because the heart isn't beating. You know the fingernails and hair keep growing, right?"

"Yeah," Lita agrees.

"So the cyanide could be gone. Even if he's found in a day or two."

"That's a stretch," Lita says.

"Well, it's reasonable, though," Nullah says, and expels a long breath.

"I can't believe we're even talking about trying to cover it up," I tell them. "I killed him. I deserve to be punished. I've made my peace with it." I get up and go to the kitchen, coming back with a beer for Nullah and a glasses of wine for Lita and me.

Lita frowns and shakes her head. "You've got to be kidding."

"Why?" I ask. "Who knows when I'll get another glass of wine?"

We drink quietly and I guess Lita and Nullah are both rolling everything around in their heads. I've had a couple hours more than they've had to get used to the idea, so it's only fair to let them ponder it.

"What about Jennifer?" Lita asks. "If you go to jail, what will happen to her?"

"I thought maybe you'd take her? It would only be for a few years. Nine or ten."

Lita's eyes widen but she says nothing. I take that as a no. I'm shocked. I really thought she'd step up, but then I should have remembered she never wanted kids. I thought it was because of the way the world is going, climate change and all, but really, she's not the maternal type. Or maybe it's just that for the past few years, she hasn't seen enough of Jennifer to really bond with her. That's a complication I didn't expect.

"Anyway," I continue, "I killed him. I'll take whatever's coming to me. It's only right."

Nullah says, "Well, there's what's legal. And then there's what's right."

"What do you mean?"

"Carly," Nullah begins, "did Derek ever tell you what happened to his first wife? How she died?"

"Yes. She drowned."

"You said he's threatened to throw you overboard before. Or, that you'd be going for a swim."

"But I think this is the first time he really meant it."

"I bet he always meant it," Lita says, and nods her head in the direction of the doors leading out onto the deck. "Just like holding you out over that rail. One of those times, he might very well drop you."

"Yeah, he meant it," Nullah continues. "His first wife drowned, all right, but the cops were suspicious. It's still an open case, and he's a person of interest."

"Person of interest?"

"Yeah. They think he did it. Just took her for a boat ride like he planned to do with you. They just don't have enough to charge him yet." Nullah takes a long swallow of his beer and sets the bottle on the coffee table. "I imagine he'd say you fell overboard in the rough weather and he couldn't find you. Even in daylight, in the waves that're out there now? You have no idea how hard it would be to find someone."

I take a couple of breaths and swirl the last bit of wine around in the glass. If I go to jail and Lita doesn't take Jennifer, where will she go? To Ontario, to live with my mother? I didn't want to live with her twenty

years ago, I don't think she's gotten any nicer since, and now she's practically an invalid besides. So, into foster care. And Derek was a suspect
in his first wife's death? I remember the convincing act he put on in the
doctor's office.

Maybe Nullah's right. There's what's legal, and there's what's right. I
swallow the rest of my wine. "Okay," I say. "How do we get him in the
water?"

Twenty-nine

Lita

It's surprising how heavy Derek is. The old expression "dead weight" takes on new meaning. Nullah and I lift him off the chair and Carly pulls it out from under him. The plan is to carry him through the family room and out onto the patio, then around to the front of the house and down the steps to the dock. It's definitely easier said than done. We don't want Carly more involved than moving the chair, but even with Nullah carrying most of the weight, my little effort is causing me to reconsider the plan.

"I have to put him down," I say before we're even out of the kitchen, and drop his legs. Nullah, who's holding him around his chest, lets him slide to the floor.

Derek groans.

I hear Carly's scream over my own. "He's waking up!"

"No, babe," Nullah says, "that's just the air coming out of his lungs because we moved him. Okay?"

"You sure?"

"I'm sure."

Carly and I exchange glances. Nullah says, "Really, Carly. Lita. It's common and natural."

"How do you know?" I ask. Then I realize there may be dark secrets in his past I'd rather not know about. "Forget I asked."

He looks puzzled, then says, "I was an auxiliary cop in New South Wales, remember? First responder."

Remember? I'm sure he's never mentioned it before. I wonder why not, and if it's really true. It must be. Nullah doesn't lie.

"Oh," Carly says.

"What's wrong, babe?" Nullah asks me. "You give up already?"

"Yeah. Um. His legs are heavy."

"He must spend quite a bit of time on the leg machines," Nullah suggests.

Is he trying to be funny? He looks pretty serious.

"I can help," Carly offers, and comes to stand next to me. "But how about this. We drop him off the deck, and then it's just a downhill drag from there."

"Drop him off the deck? It's—"

"It won't hurt him, Lita," she assures me.

"But he might get banged up. That might be suspicious, if he was supposed to have drowned or, er, had a heart attack and fell into the water."

"Good point," she admits. Now that she's quit crying, it's as if her mind is fully engaged again and she's a dispassionate observer. You'd almost think she was ordering pizza, while I think I might need Gravol even though I'm on dry land.

"He could get banged up on rocks in the water," Nullah says. "And if he's in the water for long enough before he's found, there won't be much—"

"There'll be predation," Carly agrees, nodding as she cuts off the rest of his comment.

"Sure, he might get eaten. But what if he isn't? What if they start looking around here? You know those forensics guys find the most obscure, tiny bits of evidence. A hair here. A drop of blood there. I know how rough it is out in front there. You saw it coming up here tonight, Nullah. Impossible to make sure there's no, er, nothing incriminating in that."

"Okay," Nullah says, "we wrap him up. You got a tarp, Carly?"

"Tarp? Oh, I don't know." She chews her bottom lip as she thinks about it. "No tarp, but how about the table cover? I mean the vinyl cover on the patio table?"

"How big is it?" Nullah asks.

"Well, the table is about four feet across, and the table cover goes right to the ground."

"So about ten feet in diameter. That should do, then," Nullah concludes.

"I'll go get it," I offer, and sprint for the patio door. It's locked, and there's no way I can see to unlock it. "How do you unlock this?"

"You have to use the key." Carly comes up beside me with keys, and unlocks it. I push out, welcoming the fresh air and even the rain on my face as I pull the cover off the table.

Back inside, Nullah directs us to spread it out on the floor in the area between the kitchen table and the cabinets. We accomplish that; then, between the three of us, put Derek in the middle of it and fold the vinyl up over him.

"Wait," Carly says. "If he was supposed to be taking a leak, his fly needs to be open." Without a second's hesitation, she bends over him and slides his zipper down, then sticks her hand in, coming out with his penis. "He's got an erection," she exclaims.

"Priapism. Also common," Nullah says.

"Huh!" Carly says. She's grinning. I can barely keep my wine down.

Nullah grabs a couple handfuls of vinyl, tugs, and the whole thing slides easily across the floor. He holds up at the door.

"Okay. You girls lift the far end and then I think once we're outside, Lita and I can take over," Nullah says. "You sure his wallet's in his pocket? And his cellphone? What about paperwork for the new boat?"

"Yes, all set," Carly confirms. "I'm sure he's got everything organized."

"I think maybe we should put his laptop on the boat, too," I suggest.

198   GAYLE SIEBERT

"Oh, you're right." Carly trots off toward Derek's study and in a couple of minutes, is back with the laptop bag.

"Okay," Nullah says, "so are you sure you're going to be okay on your own, Carly? We won't be back until tomorrow. Er, later today. You're going to phone Lita, say about nine? Tell her Derek's not home and can she meet you for brunch?"

"Yes. We're going to meet at the café. I'll tell my friends I've been doing fine since I quit working there. I'll say that Derek has gone to get a new boat. I'll buy a couple of pieces of cheesecake or something, enough for two people. Make a point of saying it's for when he gets home later." She looks at Nullah, gives a little nod, and says, "I won't forget."

"And if anyone points out that the weather's pretty bad to be coming home in the boat?"

"I say he might stay over another night, and also that he mentioned the storm would give the new boat a really serious sea trial," Carly says. "I know what to do, Nullah."

I tell Nullah, "She knows what to do, baby." I mean it, too. I never would've imagined her capable of all the planning and deception that went into killing Derek, or that she could go through with it. I mean, it's a terrible thing to do and when I wanted her to get rid of him, I didn't have murder in mind, but I can't help admiring her for it. The only flaw in her plan was thinking I'd take that obnoxious child. But I suppose if she went to prison and it was between me taking her and having her go into foster care, I'd probably cave. *Arghh*! Just the thought makes me cringe! Good motivation to do everything possible to make sure she gets away with it.

"I'll see you tomorrow," I tell her, and take the laptop bag from her. I hoist the strap over my shoulder crossbody style and give her one last hug before Nullah and I head out into the storm again.

We head around the front of the house, with Nullah walking backwards as he tugs the cover, and me doing my part at Derek's feet, lifting as best I can to make dragging him easier.

When we get to the trailhead, Nullah stops up and says, "I'm going to turn around. I can't back all the way down to the dock. It's downhill now, so you don't need to lift, um, your end. Just come up beside me with the flashlight."

I do as he asks. If anything, it's darker and the storm's worse now than when we came. All we need is lightning and it would be full on horror story. But as difficult as it makes this whole project, the storm is actually a good thing. In the unlikely event the cops should happen to come down here, the lashing rain will have erased any drag marks.

It also means it's unlikely there will be another boat out on the water. If there is, we'll have to continue a lot farther south than planned, at the risk of not getting it done before dawn. We don't want to be doing this in daylight. Too many eyes on too many other boats, plus a lot of these waterfront homes have telescopes and binoculars and nosey people who have nothing better to do on a Sunday morning than watch the channel.

Although it seems to take forever, we make it down the path and out onto the dock. Nullah drops the body next to Derek's boat and climbs over onto it, losing his balance for a second as the boat heaves. The wharf is the floating kind so it, too, is heaving. I toss the laptop bag onto Derek's boat, dig the Gravol out of my pocket and pop a couple, feeling the little blister pack for more. Just two left. Why didn't I buy more when I had the chance? But then, they were twice the drug store price and I planned to be sound asleep on the boat in Silva Bay long before now with only a short haul back to put our boat away in the morning. Turns out it was a lousy time to be cheap! This night can't end soon enough to suit me, but we still have a couple of hours on the water ahead of us.

Nullah reaches across, grabs one of Derek's arms, and pulls. The boat and wharf heave just as he does that. One more tug and Derek's body slides over the gunwale and hits the deck at his feet with a thud.

"Toss that on our boat, babe," Nullah says, pointing at the table cover. I fold it into an untidy bundle and flip it up onto the rear deck. Then I untie the rear mooring line and toss it to Nullah, who carefully coils it and lays it on the deck. He pulls up the bumpers, then hurriedly climbs back up on the dock.

The longer we're exposed on the wharf like this the more risk there is of us being noticed. The probability is minimal given the storm, but better plans than ours have been torpedoed by small details.

"Douse the light as soon as you can," he says, "and let's get this done." He gets on his boat and goes to the helm to start the engines while I cast off the mooring lines.

"Okay," I call out, and the boat starts away from the dock. He pilots it around to the other side of the dock and backs up to Derek's boat; I loose its bowline from the dock cleat and pass it to him. He snubs it on the ladder by the swim grid, and reaches out to take my hand and help me aboard. So far so good, but the really tricky part of the plan is still ahead.

Nullah steers the boat away from the dock, heading out to the middle of the channel with Derek's boat lurching through the waves a safe distance behind us. We're underway for ten minutes when instruments show we've reached a deep part of the channel.

"We're clear of DeCourcy Island now. Not much further to open water," Nullah says, and lets the engines idle. Much as we'd rather not announce our presence with running lights, we can't do what we need to in the dark, and Nullah turns on the stern light.

I push the bumpers over and Nullah goes astern to pull Derek's boat up close. He attaches a second rope, unties the tow rope and pulls the smaller boat alongside, walking along the gunwale to snub the tow rope to the front handrail while I wrap the second rope to another cleat. With the two boats rafted together, Nullah climbs onto the gunwale, takes the step across to the gunwale on Derek's much smaller boat and hops down onto the deck. He wastes no time in hoisting Derek's body onto the starboard gunwale, lifts his legs, and with a shove, Derek Fucking Wilton disappears over the side.

So far, so good. The most dangerous part of the operation is over. If we're discovered now, we'll say we came across Derek's boat just drifting and no one was aboard. Why were we out on the water in this storm? Stupid, I guess. But as long as it wasn't the Coast Guard, we could ask them the same question. Better to get far away from Derek's boat and not have to come up with a more believable story.

Now Nullah climbs back along the gunwale to the bow, where he unties the tow rope and tosses it to me. Derek's boat immediately swings with the current and its stern bumps up against our boat, jostling Nullah as he's making his way back. He topples forward so his upper body is on the cabin roof, his toes barely finding purchase on the edge of the gunwale. I utter a squeak of alarm. If he falls into the water between the two boats! But he seems unfazed, gets his balance again, and continues. I breathe a sigh of relief when he makes it to the aft deck.

I fix the tow rope to the starboard cleat on our boat and hand him the end. He loops it through the port handrail on Derek's boat and hands the end back to me. I take two loops around our handrail and hold on tight while Nullah unties our second rope and goes to start the motor.

Of course it doesn't start. Nullah is cursing under his breath and the motor coughs and sputters but refuses to keep running. I hear myself sigh. Nullah goes to the stern and follows the fuel line from the motor to where it feeds through an opening in the bench. He flips the top of the bench up to reveal the gas can. He jiggles it. "Fuckin' empty," he tells me. "I hope he didn't have another can in the garage that he was planning to bring."

He pulls his flashlight out of his pocket and shines a beam of light into the compartment. There's a second gas can farther in, and it's full. He mutters something that's lost in the wind as he switches the fuel line over to the fresh can and tries to start the motor again. It coughs and dies.

If the engine doesn't start soon, we may have to leave it at that. The longer we're out here, the more chance there is of other boaters coming along. Sure, it's stormy, but Nullah says we're on a commercial route and there might be marine traffic here because boats typically congregate at the south end of Dodd Narrows waiting for the tide to go through. The favorable tide is in two hours. We have to get Derek's boat away, and soon. Two boats so close together would be unusual enough to attract interest and the last thing we need is for some well-meaning member of the public coming over to see if we need help. Plus we have to go through the Narrows on the favorable tide ourselves.

The motor gives one last cough and roars to life. I breathe a sigh of relief. Nullah puts Derek's boat in gear and hurries to its stern. I reach across to grab his arm, just in case, but he makes the leap onto our boat no problem.

"Okay," he says, "let's let'er go!"

He takes the rope from me and lets the line feed off the rail. Derek's boat heads away into the storm, the engine racing with each wave that's high enough to lift the prop out of the water. It's soon far enough away we can't hear more than a dull growl over the sound of the storm, and then nothing. I coil the ropes while Nullah goes to the helm, puts the boat in gear, and we speed away. In a few minutes, he turns on our running lights and relaxes against the back of his chair. I realize that while I was nervous watching him as he did what he had to and he seemed confident and calm doing it, it must have been a terrifying experience for him.

"Dunno how long it'll keep heading into the storm," he says, "glad that's over."

"*Fucking* glad it's over," I agree. After a moment, I ask, "Did he, er, his body, um, sink right away?"

"Yeah."

When we were hatching this disposal plan, we discussed the fact bodies are sometimes never found. Sometimes they float for a while because of air in the lungs, but they can also sink to the bottom and stay there for days and even weeks if the water's cold. With luck, that's what will happen to Derek, and we're hoping currents carry him south before he's bloated enough to bob up and wash ashore or be found at sea by a boater.

Sometimes they're all or partially eaten. In the past there have been feet, still inside shoes, washed up on shore up and down the coast. Never in pairs. The person they once belonged to not identified.

As I'm running through all of this in my mind for the hundredth time, I realize disembodied feet are nothing compared to the horror of what we've just done. My stomach has been threatening to turn itself inside out for hours. Gravol is no match for this! I race to lean over the side and vomit, my stomach squeezing again and again until it's painful. Then I turn my face up to the rain and let it wash over me, cold and stinging and very welcome.

When I come back to the mate's chair, Nullah reaches across and grips my shoulder, giving it a gentle squeeze.

"Remember that discussion we had a few months ago about whether or not you needed to learn how to handle the boat?"

Now? He's going to bring that up now?

"If I fell in the chuck just then, I'd be very glad to know you could bring the boat back and fish me out." He actually laughs like we we're off on a grand adventure, and says, "You're a decent first mate, babe. I think I'll keep you."

I don't trust myself to speak. I dig out the last two Gravol tablets, and swallow them. If he thinks this was fun, I'm beginning to wonder if he has a little more in common with his biker friends than I thought.

Thirty

Carly

The cowbell over the door jingles; I push in and I'm greeted by the noisy clatter of dishes and people chatter and the aroma of cinnamon buns. The place has changed a little since I was last here. The condiments bar is now in the middle of the room, snugged up against one of the supporting pillars. There's a countertop over the bins for garbage and recyclables, with another bin on top so customers can now bus their own tables. The red checkered tablecloths are gone. The place is nearly full, so customers don't seem to mind not having tablecloths or taking their own dirty dishes to the tub.

I make my way through the tables to the counter where Ariana is busy adding more cinnamon buns to the glass display case. Without looking up, she says, "I'll be right with you," and pushes the last of the buns inside.

"Hi, Ariana," I say.

She looks up and exclaims, "Oh, Carly!" She puts the tray and tongs down and scurries around the end of the counter to put her arms around me for a hug. She releases me and says, "My god, where've you been? I thought you'd at least stop by once in a while."

"I know, I should have. It's just that I've been busy. So busy. And before you know it, weeks have gone by. You're working mornings now? How's your course going?"

"Great! My course is going great. No school on the weekends and Adeline wanted weekends to be with her family so I gladly took extra hours. I'm only here until the end of the semester then I'm going to move to the lower mainland. Closer to UBC. What about you?"

"Well, today Derek's gone off to get a new boat. He left before I even got up and he's going to be gone all day. I'm taking advantage of having the whole day to myself to meet a friend here."

"Oh, a new boat! That's awesome! Not really the best time of year for it, though."

"He says because it's off season he got a good deal and the new boat's so big storms don't bother it." I feel my face turning red as I spew out these scripted lies.

"Oh, it must be nice!"

"I guess so. I haven't seen it yet. You know men! They don't need the wife's input."

"I suppose not. Can I get you something?"

"I'm going to have an apple cinnamon muffin, and coffee. I think I'll take one of those bacon and spinach quiches before they're all gone, too. To go. Derek's favorite. So I'll have something quick and easy to warm up for him even if he's late getting home." My chest feels tight, but I manage to smile.

"Sure thing," Ariana says, and goes back behind the display case. She passes me a mug, then takes tongs and selects the muffin. "Do you want that heated?"

"Yes, please."

"You go ahead and get your coffee, then get a table while you still can." She nods at the door where another couple has come in. "You can sit at the break table in the side room if you want."

"I think I'll do that," I tell her.

"I'll bring you your muffin and your quiche in a sec."

"Thanks!" I go to the coffee bar, select the Dark Columbian pump carafe and fill my mug. Coffee in hand, I go through to the side room. There are several empty tables here, but I head for the one nearest the back kitchen entrance where there's a 'Reserved for Staff' sign posted on the wall above it.

I nod to the seniors at the next table. They're regulars and remember me, calling me by name when they say hello. I set my coffee down but remain standing to chat for a few seconds, telling them I'm not working anywhere, just retired, agreeing I'm too young to be retired but that I'm enjoying it just the same. I'm uneasy talking so much, but the more people who can say I was here this morning, acting like it's any other morning, talking about my husband being gone for the day, the better.

I tell them I'm meeting a friend and go to sit in the chair next to the wall. Holding my coffee in both hands to stop their shaking I bow my head over the mug to inhale the scent. I could almost cry. Not because I regret killing Derek, but because I don't. Or at least I'm not sorry he's gone. But taking a life? Even with good reason? What have I become?

Ariana brings my muffin with a pat of butter on a plate, and the quiche in a string-tied box. I split the muffin and slather it with butter, digging into it with gusto. I'm well into my second coffee before Lita puts in an appearance. That's Lita for you, always late. I'm not going to call her on it, though, because beautiful, always unruffled Lita looks like hell.

"What's up?" I say, loudly enough the seniors at the next table can hear me over their chatter and the banging of pans coming from the kitchen. "Rough night? You look like something the cat dragged in."

Lita's hands are shaking as she sets her mug of coffee on the table and takes the chair across from me. "You could say that," she says. "Engine trouble with the boat."

I smile. She's on script, too. We agreed they'd claim engine trouble in case anyone ever asked questions about why it took them so long to get from Silva Bay to Nanaimo. We don't expect it to come up, but you know what they say, the devil's in the details. She carefully sips her coffee, holding the mug in both hands and avoiding eye contact.

"Are you going to eat something?" I ask. "I'll go get it for you. My treat!"

"Um, no thanks, Carly," she says, color draining from her already pale face. She swallows hard a couple of times. "Didn't get much sleep last night and my stomach's still a bit rocky today."

I smile and reach across the table to give her forearm a rub. She looks as though she might throw up.

"That's too bad. I slept like a dead person last night."

She's startled. I realize that oft-used expression is horribly inappropriate now. In fact, it conjures images of Derek, sleeping in the cold darkness of the deep. No doubt that's where her thoughts went, too. She jumps to her feet and bolts for the washrooms.

Ariana comes around to clear dishes. "Where'd your friend go?"

"She's not feeling well so she went to the ladies' room," I reply. "Say, would you get me another muffin? Caramel spice this time?"

"Of course," she says, and scurries off. I go to the coffee bar for a third refill.

Only a few hours after I murdered my husband, I'm ecstatic because I can have a second muffin with no one calling me a fat, disgusting pig.

No question about it, I'm evil.

Thirty-one

Lita

It's Cinco de Mayo and Carly has organized a Mexican-themed dinner for the four of us. It's an unseasonably warm day and sunny on the patio, so being outside is pleasant. Hank and Carly sit side by side on the porch swing, hand in hand, both beaming. I've seen that look before. It's the "we just invented sex" expression. I'm sure I've had it myself at times.

I tell myself it's awesome to see Carly happy. Carly and Hank are planning on having a baby. She always wanted a husband and kids and now she'll have both again. He's always wanted kids but never found the right woman. The crazy man is so smitten with Carly he's happily taken on her obnoxious teenager. Carly's fortieth birthday is in her rear view; she wants another baby or maybe even two, but she's worried about her biological clock ticking. Which means they're in a hurry. In other words, lots of sex. Hence Hank's Cheshire Cat expression.

"So Carly, Lita tells me the subjects came off that offer, so I guess this'll be our last dinner on this patio," Nullah says. "Did you get your price?"

"Close enough. But values have gone up so much it doesn't really matter. I'm happy with it. And waterfront properties, even with drop-on beach like this, have gone up faster than anything. Having the dock turned out to be a real selling point."

"It can really come in handy," I say. Nullah gives me an odd look. I don't want to meet his gaze, and look away.

"We can go ahead and build the new house now. We got that lot we put an offer in on," Hank says. "Not waterfront, but nice ocean view so we won't miss this place too much. You guys should come take a look."

"Sure," Nullah agrees. "How about tomorrow?"

"Perfect," Hank says. "I'll show you the plans, too. See if you've got any ideas for improvement."

"Jennifer will have to change schools," Carly points out, "but I went to three different high schools and I turned out all right, so she'll be fine. She's actually looking forward to it, I think. At least she's interested in her new room. Talking about paint and carpet colors and so on. Surprising how her attitude toward me changed when she realized her father was gone for good."

"It's tough on kids, but they're resilient," Nullah says. He gets up and goes to check the salmon on the barbeque. "Nearly ready."

"Anyone need another drink?" I ask. I know I do, especially after Carly's comment about Derek being gone 'for good' and how she 'turned out all right'. I'm not sure in what universe being a murderer falls in the 'turned out all right' column. She's obviously more successful than I am at forgetting. Or more likely, she's absolved herself of blame for what she thinks was justifiable homicide. In my more reflective moments, I think it was justified, too. No question she would be dead if he wasn't, but what I struggle with is how we covered it up. Derek is often in my dreams, or rather, in my nightmares, although he's never aggressive, just sort of hovering around. He looks like he did when he was alive, and although he doesn't speak, he conveys blame and I always awake awash in guilt.

"I'll help myself," Hank says, bringing my thoughts back to the present. "In fact, I'll top up both you ladies' glasses while I'm up." He gets to his feet and disappears through the patio doors, coming back with the box of wine and a couple of Coronas, complete with lime wedges. He puts the beer on the table, then brings the box to me to fill my wineglass and does the same with Carly's.

"Thank you," I say.

Hank puts the wine box on the table, picks up the beers, and takes one to Nullah. "You said the kicker on your dinghy packed it in. I've got a used one you might be interested in."

"Oh yeah? You come across one?"

"I've had it for a while. Just remembered it. I pulled the kicker off Carly's boat back when it first came in. 9.9 horse Merc, four stroke, nice little engine. Cleaned it up and it runs good, just like new. Doubt if it was ever even used."

"Sounds perfect. But off Carly's boat? You still got that?" Nullah asks.

"Yeah. Already pulled everything that was salvageable off it ages ago, ran fresh water through the motors, sold the big one almost right away. Had no immediate takers for the kicker so I stuck it up in the mezzanine and forgot about it. Came across it last week when I was up there looking for something else. Still trying to decide if the hull's worth fixing. You saw how beat up it was."

Nullah nods. "Yeah, it took quite a beating, washing up where it was so rocky. I'm surprised you even considered repairing it."

"I had to say I'd try, at first," Hank says. "It was the only excuse I had to talk to Carly, remember." He turns and smiles at Carly.

"Godawmighty, how many times were we all together and it took you two years to ask her out?" Nullah says. "We thought you'd never get up the nerve."

"When do you ask a widow woman for a date? How soon is too soon?"

"In her case, there was no *too soon*," I mutter.

Nullah gives me a sharp look and says, "Might've been simpler if he, er, his body was found so we weren't all waiting for that."

"Some of us are still waiting for that," I point out. I look at Carly and see she's contentedly sipping her wine. If she's fretting about his body not being found or what evidence there might still be if it is found, she doesn't show it. It's like she quit thinking about him, and what happened, when he was pronounced legally dead.

I can't believe how much better she's handled this than I have. I sink back in my deck chair and lift my glass for a long swallow as the memory of that stormy night washes over me.

Nullah says, "Anyway, how many years is it and you're still fucking around pretending you're going to repair the boat? I think you could give it up. Especially now that you got that ring on her finger."

"You're right," Hank agrees. "Fact is, it's in the back corner of the yard overgrown with blackberries. I think the feral cats that are on the office doorstep every morning waiting for me to feed them, live in it."

"I've honestly forgotten you were ever planning on repairing it. Either early onset dementia or selective memory," Carly says, and giggles. "What would we do with it if it was fixed up? Is it worth anything?"

"Well, sure, it's worth something I guess, but not enough to pay for labour and materials," Hank replies.

I wish I had selective memory like Carly's, instead of reliving every moment of being an accessory after the fact, even if he deserved what he got. I manage to banish the terrible memory, collect myself, and say, "Surely you don't want it as a project, like a hobby. Not when fixing boats is your business."

"Babe, he only said he'd fix it so he could get with Carly," Nullah reminds me. "You know that."

"Busted!" Hank agrees, smiles sheepishly and takes a long swallow of his beer. "Well, it worked. So, the boat served its purpose."

"More than you will ever know," I agree.

"Okay, the salmon's done," Nullah says a little more loudly than necessary, and slides the spatulas under it to remove it to the platter.

Carly stands and says, "Great! I'll get the potato salad. I tried a new recipe, Mexican potato salad. Dijon mustard, vinegar, a hint of cumin, and finely chopped sundried potatoes. I think you guys will like it!" She bounces off through the patio doors heading for the kitchen.

"I'll make the margaritas," Hank says, and follows her in.

I take a seat at the table and open my contribution, the corn salad that was the closest thing to a Mexican salad available at the deli.

Nullah brings the salmon to the table, sets it down, and sits next to me. He puts a hand on my shoulder and gives it a rub. From the kitchen comes the sound of the blender whirring into action.

"You okay, babe?" Nullah asks quietly. "Those memories, again?"

He knows me so well at times it seems he reads my thoughts. As unbelievably sweet it is to have such a connection with this beautiful man, there are times I wish he couldn't read me so easily. This is one of those times. I take a deep breath and nod.

"I know it does no good to say this, but try not to think about it."

"I *am* trying."

"I know you are." He leans over and lifts my chin for a kiss. "Being with her always seems to remind you. Maybe we should quit seeing them."

"But Hank's your mate."

"Yeah. So are you. And it isn't good, you fixating about that night. You're the most important thing in my life. I don't like how this eats away at you."

I kiss him again, then sink back in my chair, turn my face up to the sky and watch the clouds changing shape as they ride across invisible currents. He strokes my forearm.

"Nullah?"

"Yeah?"

"About that night. Something I've been wondering about and I really have to ask you. About dead bodies—was your experience with them—that is, were you really an auxiliary cop?"

When he doesn't answer, I sit upright and study his profile. He doesn't face me. Instead, he lowers his chin to look down as if he's just noticed his sandals are on the wrong feet.

Carly and Hank come out with the potato salad, glasses, and the pitcher of margaritas, and deposit everything on the table with a clatter.

"Nullah?" I persist.

He turns his head to face me and says, "Yes."

Something about his lips tightly pressed together and his eyes narrowed leads me to believe the man I thought could not tell a lie is doing just that. And something about the set of his jaw tells me I shouldn't ask again.

"Okay?" he asks.

Is it okay? I don't know. Do I really want to know more? I realize I don't. I manage to summon a smile and answer, "Okay."

"Good." Nullah breathes out loudly, sits up straight and turns to the others to say, "Hey, Hank, about tomorrow. We can't go check out that lot of yours after all. Turns out we have a conflict."

Don't miss out!

Visit the website below and you can sign up to receive emails whenever Gayle Siebert publishes a new book. There's no charge and no obligation.

https://books2read.com/r/B-A-EAZM-VMGOC

BOOKS 2 READ

Connecting independent readers to independent writers.

Did you love *The Feeder*? Then you should read *Katawasis Girls*[1] by Gayle Siebert!

[2]

A new job in another town seems like the answer to a prayer. But taking it could be a fatal decision.

Lindy Larsen's job at Western Savings & Loan is what keeps her ranch afloat, so when she's offered a promotion she accepts, even though the bigger paycheque means moving to the remote town of Katawasis Lake.

Only days into her new job, Lindy runs afoul of the manager's unconventional rules. She has no choice but to do as he asks, but can't shake the feeling he's hiding something, and it may not be legal. The regional bank auditors are suspicious too, and recruit Lindy in a sting operation. Then there's a spate of bodies found in the lake and the victims

---

1. https://books2read.com/u/mddzVZ

2. https://books2read.com/u/mddzVZ

all have one thing in common: ties to the bank. Lindy finds herself in the middle of something that's more than fraud and bigger than just the bank manager. She has stumbled into a tangled maze of criminal activity more widespread than they realized and she's attracted the attention of some very dangerous people.

Lindy has a target on her back. Will she be the next floating corpse? Read more at https://www.gaylesiebert.com.

Also by Gayle Siebert

Lindy Larsen
After The Dance
Katawasis Girls
The Bones Below

Lisa Rogney
Call Me Lisa
Wembly

Secrets
The Bear Mountain Secret
The Spirit Bear Secret
The Dark River Secret

Standalone
Where The Mule Grazed
The Feeder

Watch for more at https://www.gaylesiebert.com.

About the Author

Gayle has always loved horses, reading, and writing. She has been a trail rider, barrel racer, and dressage rider. Now retired after more than 3 decades as an insurance adjuster, she lives on a horse farm near Nanaimo, British Columbia, Canada, writes, reads, and yes, still rides.

Read more at www.gaylesiebert.com.